PRINTHOUSE BOOKS PRESENTS

I0614828

Pulsations of a Heartbeat

I gave her my last breath.

Fiction

Lorenzo 'el Gee' Gladden

VIP INK Publishing Group, Inc.
Atlanta, GA.

I gave her my last breath.

Printed in the USA

Cover art designed by SK7.

Editor: Shelby Oates

Published: 11-26-2015

Isbn – 978-0-9965-701-3-8

Library of Congress Cataloging-in- Publication Data

#2015953397

Lorenzo 'el Gee' Gladden

1.Drama 2.Suspense 3.Urban Lit 4.Romance

When a man finds himself dating or in relationships with the same type of women repeatedly, he has fallen into his comfort zone. He knows how that woman thinks, expects to be treated and most of all, he knows how she will treat him. At times this becomes boring and stagnant. Once this happens, it is time to step outside of the box.

Pulsations of a Heartbeat: *I gave her my last breath* is a journey into the life of Kevin Montgomery. Kevin is a successful Real Estate investor that has made huge waves in Atlanta, Georgia. His chosen type of woman is a corporate woman or an entrepreneurially minded woman. Finding no luck with these women, he steps outside of his comfort zone when he meets Brittany.

Brittany is an exotic dancer with a dream. Against all reservations, Kevin takes a chance on her. Like he does with every woman, he gives Brittany his all. How does a woman with a different mentality than normal women react to this? How will she react when he gives her everything? The heart is fragile and if it becomes constricted, it will slowly come to a halt and there will be no more breath to give.

I gave her my last breath.

Dedicated to
Monica N. Oliver
No matter what life is throwing at
you, never let it change who you
are.

Lorenzo 'el Gee" Gladden

Pulsations of A Heartbeat

I gave her my last breath.

VIP INK Publishing Group, Inc.
Atlanta, GA.

I gave her my last breath.

Table of Contents

Lorenzo Gladden

1
Kev and Rich

Flowers were blooming.
The leaves returned to the trees.
Birds soared through the air
singing their beautiful songs.
Springtime in Atlanta, Georgia had
finally arrived. Women filled the
salons and spas to shed their winter
fur. New attitudes were formed in
the aftermath of Yule Tide
heartbreak and broken New Year's
resolutions. All which was dead
could now come back to life. For
many men and women, spring
signified new life.

In life, people build
relationships and bonds. There is a
reason for the crossing of two
paths. As the old saying goes,
People enter your life for a reason,

a season, or a lifetime. It is up to said person to figure out which one. Choose the wrong one and the end result could be severe.

On a warm Monday evening, Kevin Montgomery walked into the Run N' Shoot in downtown Atlanta for his weekly dose of basketball. Kevin stood 6'2" with a muscular frame coated by a light brown complexion. His bald head shined as the overhead lights beamed off it. Versace shades covered his dark brown eyes. In his black Air Jordan t-shirt, red Jordan basketball shorts and red and black elevens, Kevin walked and scanned the area to find a pick-up game. He noticed that on the far end of the gym there was a game going on but only a few people sitting on the sidelines waiting for it to end. He walked over and put his bag down.

"What's up, Bruh?" Kevin greeted a dark skinned stranger

with a long beard sitting on the side watching the game. "Do you know who has next game?"

"I got next."

"You got your five?"

"I need one more."

"Can I get a run?"

"Yeah."

"I'm Kev," Kevin extended his fist to the stranger.

"Rich," he replied as he gave Kev a pound.

"What the competition look like?"

"There're a few players out there. You see the brother in the blue shorts? His squad is winning, but he's doing all the work."

"So what you're saying is that if they win, all we have to do is shut him down and we got it."

"Precisely."

As the game neared the end, Kev and Rich stood up to begin stretching. They continued to shoot the breeze while readying for their upcoming game. Game point was scored. After a few minutes of friendly trash talk, the winning team took a break to catch their breath and rehydrate. The five new players took the court to shoot around.

The plan to shut down the winning team's leading scorer proved effective and gave Rich's and Kev's team a dominant victory. They held the court for five straight games on the strength of Kevin's passing and Rich's shooting. Before long, fatigue set in and the 30 year olds finally went down to a team of younger players.

"Good run," Kev complimented as he wiped his face with a towel.

"You too, My Brother. You must've played ball in school."

"I played in high school and college. What about you?"

"I played in high school up in N-Y."

"Why not in college?"

"Young and dumb. I got into some trouble and did a five year bid. After I got out, I went to college, but my basketball years were far behind me."

"I can feel that. At least you had the sense to learn from your mistake and did something positive when you got out. Not too many brothers do that."

"While in prison, I realized that my life was worth so much more and I didn't want to let the mistakes I made mold me into a product of the system."

"That's a good attitude to have. Wait a minute…you said you played ball in New York. Right?"

"That's right."

"You don't speak like the New Yorkers I'm used to."

"I'm from Niagara Falls."

"Well then that explains it. What did you major in?"

"I got my BS in Marketing and my MBA with a concentration in Finance both from Niagara University. What about you?"

"I have my BA in Secondary Education from NC State. I taught high school English for five years. I was getting ready to begin my graduate studies when I ran into one of my boys from college while down here visiting some family. He was into real estate. To make a long story short, I linked up with him and he showed me how to flip houses. The next thing I know, I moved from Fayetteville to the A, went to real estate school and the rest is history. He introduced me to some good business contacts and I made some of my own in the process. I made my salary from my five years teaching and my first year doing real estate."

"That's what I like to hear…a black man doing

something positive with his life. I tried to go the corporate route but when you're an ex-con, the establishment is not trying to hear that. I didn't let it get me down though. I took some money I had saved, bought me a used truck, a pressure washer, some detailing supplies and started a mobile detail business. Now I have my own spot in Buckhead."

"With all this pollen coming down, I need to bring my car through and let you hook it up."

"Are you getting ready to walk outside?"

"Yeah."

"I'll get you a business card."

The two men continued to talk as they walked toward the parking lot. By sheer coincidence they were parked right beside each other.

"Where you at?" Rich asked as he surveyed the parking lot.

"I'm in the black Maserati beside the white Porsche."

"I'm the white Porsche."

"Business must be booming."

"I'm blessed. I just picked her up a couple of months ago. I have a pretty good relationship with the owners of Imports Atlanta. Nasir called me when it came on the lot and said that he had a car just for me. What model is that you driving?"

"That's the 2015 Ghibli Q4."

Rich opened his car door, pulled his wallet from under the seat and handed Kev a business card.

"When is the best time to come in?"

"You already know Fridays and Saturdays are busy because of

the weekend, but any time you want to come…just call me and I'll fit you in."

"One of the guys in my office is getting married Saturday and we're taking him out Friday night for his bachelor party."

"Say no more. Call me first thing Friday morning and I'll set you up."

"I really appreciate that. Here's my card. If you're ever looking to buy a house or want to do some investing in real estate give me a call."

"That sounds like a plan. I do have some money put away that I want to do something with."

"I can show you how to take that money and make you some more money. How does that sound?"

"Like music to my ears."

"I'm leaving tomorrow to go out of town to meet with an investment group based in Miami.

I gave her my last breath.

I'll be back Thursday morning.
Let's do lunch or dinner and we
can talk some business."

"It will definitely have to
be dinner."

"When you figure out what
time is good for you, text me and
I'll have my assistant set us up
somewhere."

"That sounds like a plan."

"Alright, Rich. I'll be
expecting to hear from you."

"Indeed you will. Have a
blessed night, my brother."

"Same to you.

———————

The week coasted by and
Kevin was just getting back to
Atlanta from his business
excursion to Florida. He was on a
natural high because of the trip's
success. It was exactly what he
needed to make the jump from
residential into commercial.

Kevin pulled into his driveway around 3:30pm that afternoon. Having worked hard to achieve success, Kevin's residence was on West Paces Ferry Rd. For those that are not familiar with that area, it takes money to reside there. Fortunately for Kevin, his experience and connections in real estate and rehabbing properties gave him a leg up over his neighbors that paid market price.

Being single, he didn't need a huge home, but he did want a nice sized space for when he was ready to start his family. Twenty thousand square feet was just right. His home was a three bedroom, four bathroom, single level abode with a finished basement. Dark bamboo floors spread throughout the entirety of the structure. One of the bedrooms was off of the basement with its own bathroom. The rest of the basement was designated as his man cave.

I gave her my last breath.

The Master bedroom was
on the main level with the other
bedroom. It featured a private bath
and four huge closets with three-
way mirrors in each: One for
casual wear, one for dress and
formal wear, one for business attire
and one for shoes.

With the culinary skills that
Kevin possessed, naturally, the
kitchen was laid. It was equipped
with all stainless appliances
including a six burner island stove.
There was a huge sliding glass
door off of the kitchen that led to
the backyard.

In the confines of the six
feet tall privacy fence was a
stunning in-ground swimming pool
and Jacuzzi. Across from the pool
was a custom built barbecue grill
and bar area with two beer taps.
With the help of Atlanta's top
interior designers and landscape
artists, Kevin's home was fit for a
king but still awaiting a queen.

As he walked in and put his bag down, he received a text from his assistant telling him that his dinner with Rich was set for 8:30pm at Ruth Chris in Buckhead. He relayed the message to Rich. After receiving his affirmation, Kev changed into basketball shorts and a tank top then retired to his man cave to relax. The events of his trip had taken a toll on him. While trying to catch up on one of his favorite television shows, Kevin fell asleep.

Kevin jumped out of his slumber fearful that he'd overslept. The time on his watch displayed 6:59pm. He turned off the television and walked upstairs to take a shower and begin getting dressed for the evening. After his shower, he wrapped a towel around his waist and walked into the closet that housed his business apparel. He rifled through his many custom tailored suits trying to select one.

Alexander McQueen was the designer of the evening. The suit was a darker shade of cobalt blue. When it came to dressing, Kevin was very anal about it. He never mixed designers. For that night, everything was Alexander McQueen: suit, shirt, belt, and shoes.

Kevin never considered himself a vain or conceited person, but he did believe in looking good whenever he stepped out. Standing in front of the mirror in the closet, he surveyed his clothing. To the left of the mirror were four drawers. He pulled out the first one. It contained his watches that he wore with his business attire. His favorite time piece was Rolex, but for the night he chose a low key, all black Citizen Eco to match his belt and shoes.

By the time Kevin finished putting himself together, it was 8 o'clock. He sprayed on a subtle amount of Creed then headed towards the front door. At the door was a small stand with a drawer. That was where he kept the keys to his three cars. His everyday driver was a 2013 Silver Camaro SS. This was so he wouldn't put all those city miles on the Maserati. His third car was a black on black 2013 Mercedes G500. Kevin grabbed the keys to the Maserati and headed to Buckhead. Rich was already in place when Kevin arrived wearing black linen pants, matching shirt and leather loafers.

"Greetings my Nubian brother," Rich extended his hand as Kevin approached. "How was the trip?"

"Lucrative, yet tiring. I hope I didn't keep you waiting too long."

"I actually just arrived myself."

"Good. Our reservation isn't until 8:30. We have about 10

minutes. Let's get a drink and wait for our table."

"That sounds good to me."

The two men took a seat at the bar. A short, small framed yet well-built Latina with her silky black hair pulled into a ponytail placed beverage napkins in front of them.

"How are you handsome gentlemen doing this evening?"

"Doing well," Kevin replied.

"I'm blessed," Rich answered.

"That's good to hear. My name is Mercedes. We have a fully stocked bar, ice cold beers and a great wine list. What may I get for you this evening?"

"What do you have in a good Riesling?" Kevin inquired.

"Chateau Davenport is my favorite. We also have…"

"I'll have that. A good friend of mine owns that vineyard."

"And for you, Sir?"

"Stella Artois."

"Excellent choices."

Shortly after the drinks were received, the men were notified that their table was available. Kevin paid the bar tab and followed the hostess to the table.

"Here you go gentlemen," the hostess began as she placed the menus on the table. "Kari will be right over to take great care of you."

"Thank you."

"Shall we get down to business?" Rich asked.

"Straight to the point…I like that."

"No disrespect, but If I'm in a place like this, I'd rather it be with a woman. Since this is about potentially making money, I'm cool."

"I can respect that. Now, you have a couple of options. You can buy and sell or you can buy and rent."

"Buy and rent?"

Before Kevin could answer the question the server approached the table. Kara was a slim framed black female that looked to be in her early to mid-twenties with a caramel complexion. Her hair was cut into a bob and her hands were perfectly French manicured.

"Good evening gentlemen. My name is Kari and I'll be taking great care of you this evening."

"Thank you, Kari. Before you go into the Chef's specials, could you bring my associate and I another round then give us about twenty minutes. We have some business to discuss before we order. I promise you it will be worth it for you."

"No problem at all. What are you drinking?"

"I'm drinking the Château Davenport Riesling and my associate is drinking Stella."

"Would you like for me to put in an appetizer with those drinks?"

Looking at Rich, "I like her. She's about her business. Do you eat calamari?"

"I love calamari."

"Good. Bring us an order of calamari and the crab stuffed mushrooms."

"Excellent choices. I'll put those in and bring your drinks."

"Thank you, Kari." Looking back to Rich, "Where were we?"

"Buying and renting."

"Ahh yes…that is when you buy a property but instead of selling it, you rent it out."

"Interesting. Which option did you start with?"

"Before I started building my rental portfolio, I went with the first option. That allowed me to build my capital."

"If I chose option one, what is the first step?"

"After all the particulars are in place and we have a signed business agreement, the first thing I will do is send my locators out to find you a viable property. When you first start out, you want something simple. My suggestion is a 3 bedroom, 1.5 to 2 bath brick ranch style home. It's the easiest to flip."

"Would I be selling it to the general public?"

"That is one option or you can sell to another investor building his or her portfolio."

"How long does the process take?"

"Once we find the right property and the due diligence is

done, the process takes roughly 90-120 days. I usually have a project manager oversee the projects, but since this will be your first time, I serve as project manager."

"You don't have to do that. You seem to have a proven system."

"No problem at all…in fact, I insist."

"I'm with you so far. What's the next step? Will I be purchasing the property with my own money?"

"That depends on you. If you have that type of money to spend, it will make you more money at the end. If not the only thing you will have to provide is the earnest money for the property. Then we use hard money for the purchase and the rehab."

"What is hard money?"

"For these projects we use hard money banks. They aren't your typical banks. The money they loan is short term and high interest."

Rich raised an eyebrow when he heard the term high interest.

"I know that you've been taught that when you finance anything you want to get the lowest interest rate possible and you will once you start building your rental portfolio. Are you still with me?"

"I'm hanging on as best I can. This is a different element for me. I'm sure you can break it down further for me if we move forward. What I want to know is how I make money."

"Once we finish everything that we set out to do to the property in the rehab process, the value of the property changes and it's now at market value. The market value is determined by the finished property, the property value of the area and the current market."

"I get that part but I need some numbers."

"Let's say we purchase a foreclosure for $30,000. We put another $20,000 in the rehab. This brings the market value of the property to $100,000. Once we sell the property, the buy bank pays the hard money back for what was put into the investment and you get the difference minus my company fees. To make a long scenario short, you make close to 40,000 on your first flip."

"Just like that?"

"It's that simple. Because you have a business and money that you have put aside, that makes you liquid. I'll have no problem getting the hard money loan."

"What kind of credit score do I need?"

"When you're liquid, credit score means nothing."

"That's a lot to take in. I need to take some time to think it over."

"Take all the time you need. I've been doing this for almost 10 years. I'm not going anywhere anytime soon. As a matter of fact, I got a call from an investor looking to buy two rehabbed properties for his rental portfolio. One of those could be yours. I have the particulars for what he wants and it could make you around $30,000 in 3-4 months depending on the rehab."

"That would make for a very merry Christmas."

"Kwanza and Hanukkah," Kevin laughed.

"When do you need an answer?"

"If you want to get in for the investor I have now, I need an answer by Sunday evening. I'm sending the locators out first thing Monday morning."

"I'll have an answer for you on Sunday."

"I'll have the paperwork ready for you to go over and sign on Tuesday."

"How do you know I'll say that I'm in?"

"I just met you four days ago and I feel that you are a smart man. When you leave here tonight you are going to research me and KM Enterprises, run the numbers on your own, see that I'm reputable and the numbers work and you'll be calling me on Sunday."

"To quote my man Master Yoda: *'Strong in this one, the confidence is'*."

The two men shared a laugh then ordered their meals. They continued to talk business until the meal came. As they were eating, Rich spied a young lady sitting at the bar.

"Do you see that queen sitting at the bar?"

"Yes indeed. She's gorgeous."

"Excuse me for a moment. I have to introduce myself to her."

"Don't hurt ya'self."

Rich excused himself and walked to the bar to greet the young lady that was sitting alone. She was a picture of elegance. Her brownish-black hair hung long and straight past her shoulders. The form fitting black dress she wore hugged the contour of her body. The split in the side revealed a pair of beautiful, unblemished, crossed legs.

"Excuse me my queen, I was sitting there with my business associate and I noticed that you've been sitting here alone for quite some time."

"I was supposed to meet my date here. He's late as usual."

"Forgive my forwardness, but I would never leave a woman with your beauty and essence waiting for me."

"That's sweet of you to say."

"My name is Richard, but you can call me Rich."

"It is a pleasure to meet you Rich. I'm Melissa."

"I have to get back to my business meeting, but if your date doesn't show or you're just looking for something real, don't hesitate to give me a call." Rich pulled out his wallet and handed Melissa a business card.

"Thank you. It was nice meeting you."

"Likewise."

Rich returned to the table.

"How did it go?"

"She said she was waiting on someone. I gave her my card and told her to give me a call."

"I like that. You didn't press. You're letting her come to you."

"I may not know anything about real estate but women…that's my area of expertise."

"I'll drink to that."

———————————

Once business was adjourned and the meal was over, Kev and Rich went their separate ways for the evening. Kevin returned home to call it an early night due to the events that were on the horizon for the following night.

2
Sapphire

In every city across the country, Friday night is when millions of people let their hair down to forget the woes of the work week. The Buckhead area of Atlanta is where it all goes down. Kevin's destination for the night was Club Ebony. It was Atlanta's hottest gentlemen's club. This was where the real ballers, athletes, and entertainers go to play. Kevin wasn't a strip club patron, but one of his investors was getting married and Club Ebony was where his best man chose to have his bachelor party.

The clock struck midnight as Club Ebony was just getting

ready to get into high gear. The DJ had the club on lean as the ladies were shaking ass and titties everywhere. Even though Kevin was out of his element, he managed to have a good time. He sat and watched as his investors and other colleagues acted like stone cold idiots. Most of them were married men which meant they didn't get out of the house much. When they did, they made the most of every opportunity.

Kevin sat in their VIP area sipping Hennessey and surveying the scene. From where they were positioned, he had a good view of the stage. The lights went low and a blue spotlight hit the pole. *Meeting in my Bedroom* by Silk, blared through the club's sound system. The DJ called Sapphire to the main stage. From behind a shear curtain, an angel appeared. This being had a light complexion that would put one in the mind of

Nivea. Kevin removed himself from his party and made his way to the stage and took a seat.

Now that she was in full view, he could really check her out. Despite the six inch stilettos, she couldn't have been more than 5'1". Sapphire had a slim body with a slightly visible six pack. Her hair was pulled into a ponytail starting high off the back of her head. The remaining hair was curly and extended to the right between her shoulder blades. A straight cut bang fell across her forehead about a half inch above her eyes. An electric blue bikini top covered her perky B cups while the matching G-string was swallowed by her ass that was as round as an onion. It looked like it didn't belong on a girl with her body size, but it fit just right.

Kevin sat in a trance as he watched her move up and down the pole. The club stage was packed with guys throwing ones, but he felt like he was the only one there. There were times when Sapphire's eyes were locked with his. When dancers are on stage, they often make it a point to tease every man surrounding the stage. For the remainder of her first song and the second song, Sapphire worked the stage and all the guys in attendance. On the third song, she took her place right in front of Kevin. For the entirety of the song, she twisted, jiggled and gyrated her flawless, naked body in front of him. Not realizing it, Kevin had not placed one bill on the stage. Once the song was over, Sapphire rounded up her mountain of dollar bills and left the stage.

Kevin gathered his thoughts and walked to the bar. He sat at the bar staring at his drink. A voice from behind him spoke into his ear.

"You don't come to strip clubs often," Sapphire whispered. "Do you?"

"What makes you say that?" He questioned after turning around.

He was surprised to see that it was Sapphire. She positioned herself right between his legs.

"Because when a girl is on stage dancing for you, you're supposed to tip her."

"I'm so sorry," Kevin took a wad of ones out of his pocket and handed them to the dancer, "I was just mesmerized by you."

"It's okay. I'll forgive you this time."

"Can I buy you a drink?"

"I don't usually accept drinks from customers, but I'll make an exception this time."

"Why do I feel like you say that to all the guys?"

"It's true. Some of these guys feel that if they buy you a

drink, you owe them something. I may be a dancer, but I'm not that type of girl."

"Why accept one from me?"

"I can tell you're not like all of these other guys."

"How can you tell?"

"Follow me and I'll answer that question."

Kevin grabbed his drink as Sapphire grabbed his hand and led him to a secluded area where they could talk without screaming at each other. The room had a couch and a couple of chairs in it. Sapphire sat Kevin down on the couch and straddled his lap.

"I'm sorry," Kevin began, "I didn't ask for a private dance."

"This isn't for that. This is just a place where we can sit and talk."

"I don't want to keep you from making your money."

"I'll manage. Now what was your question?"

"How can you tell I'm not like any other guy in here?"

"First of all, look at how you're dressed. Every guy in here has on jeans, t-shirts and hats. You have on a tailored Armani suit."

"How do you know its Armani?"

"Trust me…I know my designers."

"Touché."

"What brought you in tonight? Let me guess…a bachelor party?"

"That is correct. You're really good at reading people."

"I'm just observant. I saw you over in the VIP."

"Oh…so you were checking me out."

"Maybe…maybe not."

"I know you hear this all of time, but what is a woman as

beautiful as yourself doing in a place like this?"

"That's a long story."

"Could I convince you to tell me that story over dinner?"

"I don't usually go out with customers."

"I can respect that so I tell you what," Kevin reached into his jacket pocket and pulled out a chrome business card holder with his initials engraved on it. "Here's my card. If you'd like to take me up on my offer for dinner, give me a call. If not, I understand and it's cool."

Sapphire tucked the card into her bosom then removed herself from his lap. Kevin stood up and reached into his pocket, pulled out a sizeable wad of cash and peeled off a one hundred dollar bill. He handed Sapphire the bill.

"What's this for? I didn't even dance for you."

"In my world, time is money. Thank you for your time."

Kevin left Sapphire standing in the room confused yet intrigued. No man had ever given her money in the club without her having to work for it.

The night went on. Kevin and his friends helped the groom-to-be enjoy his last night as a single man. As the gathering wound down, the guys from Kevin's party started thinning out. As he exited the club, he heard a familiar voice call to him. He stopped and turned to the right. Sapphire was coming out of the side exit to the building. She was smiling as she approached him.

"Are you heading home?" she asked.

"Yeah...can't be out all night. I won't make it to the wedding tomorrow."

"I just wanted to say thank you."

"For what?"

"It's refreshing to meet a guy that has more than one thing on his mind when he steps through those doors. For once it was nice to talk and have a real conversation."

"We barely talked, though."

"Trust me," Sapphire laughed, "in that building, what we had was a real conversation."

"Then I guess after the conversation we have over dinner, you're going to be sending me flowers."

"Really now?"

"If you don't believe me, try me."

"Maybe I will."

"You have my card. Like I said, if you're up to it, give me a call."

Sapphire wrapped her arms around Kevin and gave him a hug.

"My name is Brittany. It was nice to meet you, Mr. Montgomery."

The two parted ways. Kevin headed home to get some sleep before the wedding. After he showered, he sat up in his bed thinking about Brittany. Never in his life had he ever thought about asking out a stripper, but he felt there was something different about her. Just as he was about to plug the charger into his phone, it rang. He didn't recognize the number. He started to ignore it, but he decided to answer it.

"Hello?" Kevin answered.

"I hope I didn't wake you," the voice on the other end responded. "This is Brittany."

"You didn't wake me. I was lying down, but I wasn't asleep."

"I know this is going to sound corny, but I couldn't stop thinking about you."

I gave her my last breath.

"I was actually thinking about you, too."

"Would you have called me if you had my number?"

"Probably not."

"Why?"

"I wouldn't want you to think I was stalking you."

"So you think I'm stalking you?"

"Of course not," Kevin laughed. "It's different for guys. I wouldn't want to give you the wrong idea."

"Just checking," Brittany giggled.

"What are you still doing up?"

"A dancer's life is equal to a vampire's life. I'm so wound up on Red Bulls and adrenaline when I get home, I don't usually fall asleep until the sun comes up."

"I can understand that. I used to be a night owl, but the way business has been going lately, I have to be up and at'em early."

"I used to be a morning person until I started dancing."

"How long have you been dancing?"

"Off and on for seven years…more off than on. J-Rock that runs the club is a good friend of mine. Whenever I get into a bind and need some quick cash, he lets me drop in and dance."

"What brought you back this time?"

"I was in school but tuition went up, my job laid me off and my car went out on me. I needed to get back on my feet so I had to do what I had to do. Feel me?"

"I feel you. What were you going to school for?"

"I want to be an esthetician so I can open my own spa one day."

"Well…when you get on your feet and are ready to open that

spa, I can help you find a building."

"Your card says real estate investment specialist. What exactly do you do?"

"I mostly flip houses."

"So you do what they do on *Flip this House*."

"In a nutshell, but what I do is nowhere near as dramatic."

Kevin and Brittany talked for about three hours.

"You getting sleepy on me?" Brittany asked when she noticed the long pauses between replies.

"I am, but I'm enjoying our conversation."

"That's cool because I'm winding down myself. I'll let you get some sleep."

"I would say I'll call you tomorrow, but by the time I finish with the wedding and the reception, you'll be at work."

"What are you doing Sunday?"

"My day is free."

"I don't dance on Sundays. Maybe we can get together."

"That sounds like a plan. What time is a good time to call you?"

"Any time after one o'clock is good."

"Then I'll talk to you Sunday."

"Enjoy the wedding."

"You have a good night at work."

———————————

It was a beautiful, spring Sunday in Atlanta. The temperature was a little chilly, but the sun shined bright in a cloudless sky. Despite the shenanigans of the past couple of nights, Kevin made it to service at his church. After church he hit the gym for his daily dose of cardio and light weightlifting. By the time he got home it was around 1:30pm. It was time for him to call Brittany.

"Hello?" Brittany answered.

"I hope I didn't wake you."

"Who is this?"

"It's Kevin."

"Hey! I didn't recognize your number. I forgot to save it in my phone the other night."

"That's okay. Did you have a good night last night?"

"It was a little slow for a Saturday, but I managed. I left earlier than usual. To be honest, I was anticipating seeing you today and I didn't want to be tired."

"That's good to hear. I have a good day planned for you."

"Really?"

"Yes. What time can you be ready?"

"I've been up for a couple of hours. I've showered already.

All I have to do is get dressed. Give me about an hour."

"That's perfect. I just got home from the gym. I have to shower and get dressed myself."

"What should I wear?"

"Jeans and a shirt is cool…oh yeah…wear some sneakers."

"Are you picking me up or would you like for me to meet you?"

"If it's okay with you, I can pick you up. I don't have a problem with that. Where do you live?"

"I live in Marietta. I'll text you the address."

"That's perfect. You're close to where we're going."

"Where are we going?"

"If I tell you…that would ruin the surprise."

"I guess I'll have to wait then."

"I'll see you in an hour."

"I'm looking forward to it."

Kevin hung up the phone and headed into the Master bathroom to shower. Once showered, he ventured to his casual closet and selected a pair of light blue Polo jeans and a royal blue and white horizontal striped Polo Rugby shirt. From his shoe closet, Kevin chose his white and Carolina blue Jordan 11's with the Carolina blue laces.

The only time Kevin wasn't too anal about designers was when he wore jeans and sneakers. He has always had a thing for Retro Jordan's and Air Force Ones. His parents couldn't afford to buy them for him when he was a kid. As a struggling college student, they were still out of his price range. Even when he became a teacher, they didn't fit into his budget. Once he started making money through real estate, he began building his collection. He had almost every style of Jordan and Air Force Ones in an array of colors.

After Kevin got dressed, he went outside to wipe down the Maserati. Once that task was completed, he headed toward Cobb County to pick up Brittany. When he pulled into her apartment complex and parked, he laughed to himself. The apartments weren't run down or in a bad neighborhood. They just reminded him of how he was living when he first started out in Atlanta. As a matter of fact, his first apartment complex made this one look like expensive condos.

Kevin got out of the car and walked upstairs to Brittany's third floor apartment. When he knocked on the door, a dog on the other side of it started to yelp. Brittany opened the door with her teacup Yorkie in her arms. She wore dark, denim jeans and a hunter green sweatshirt displaying the letters USA on the front, a classic Express item. On her feet was a pair of black, green and grey Nike Air Max 95's. Brittany's hair was long and curly.

"Hey Kevin," she greeted. "Did you have trouble finding me?"

"No trouble at all. I'm pretty familiar with this area. I've done a couple of projects close by."

"Come on in. I have to put CoCo in her kennel and we can go."

Kevin stood by the door as Brittany put her dog away then darted into her bedroom.

While standing in her bedroom doorway, "Hat or no hat?"

"Leave the hat. I like your hair like that and I can see your eyes."

Brittany smiled as she tossed the hat back into her room. They left the apartment and walked downstairs. Before they were on ground level, Kevin hit the button for his alarm. The alarm beeped once and the lights flashed.

"You drive a Maserati?" Brittany asked with wide eyes.

"Yes. She's just one of my babies."

"You sure all you do is real estate?"

"That's all I do. Everything about me is 100% legal and legit."

Kevin opened the passenger door for Brittany. As he walked around the back of the car, he observed her looking around inside the car.

"I would've unlocked your door, but I didn't want to touch anything."

"That's okay," Kevin chuckled. "Your intentions were good."

"So…where are we going?"

"Just sit back and ride. I promise you, you're in good hands."

Kevin fiddled around on the touchscreen in the dash. After about three or four touches, music flowed through the speakers and they were off to their destination. Five minutes into the ride, his phone rang and Rich's name popped up on the screen. He pressed the button to answer it.

"Rich, what's up?"

"Nothing but blessings my brother," Rich answered. "I didn't catch you at a bad time, did I? It sounds like you're driving.

"I'm with a beautiful young lady and we're enjoying this beautiful Sunday afternoon."

"That's love."

"I'm hoping this is a good news call."

"Indeed it is. I've given it much thought since Friday and I was calling to tell you that I'm ready."

"Sounds great. I'll have my assistant draw up the contract tomorrow and I'll bring them by your shop on Tuesday. How does that sound?"

"That sounds great. Let's make this money."

"That's what I'm hoping for. I'm not going to hold you. Enjoy your time with your lady friend."

"I'll need some information from you for the contract, but I can get that in the morning."

"Alright, my brother. Be blessed."

"You as well." Kevin turned to Brittany, "I'm sorry about that. I don't usually take calls when I'm out, but I was expecting that one."

"No worries at all."

"That was Rich. He's my newest investor."

"He sounds like he's excited."

"He should be. He's getting ready to make a lot of money."

"I'd be excited, too."

Ten minutes later, Kevin and Brittany arrived at Fun City. Fun City was one of those places that had mini golf, go carts, batting cages and a huge arcade with a laser tag arena inside.

"I've driven by this place numerous times and have always wanted to come," Brittany explained.

"I love this place. Whenever life starts to get out of control, I come out here and act like a big kid. It keeps me sane. What do you want to do first?"

"Definitely go carts!"

"Loser buys dinner?"

"Challenge accepted."

For three and a half hours Brittany and Kevin ran around Fun City like two grown kids. From the go carts they moved to mini golf then to the laser tag arena. From there they went into the arcade where they played air hockey, Skee Ball and any other game that would win tickets for them.

Night was falling when Brittany and Kevin finally exited the building. Atop Brittany's head were a pair of springy, alien antennae's and she carried a rather large stuffed panda. Kevin was dribbling a Georgia Tech basketball. When they got to the car he opened the back door and placed the teddy bear on the back seat and placed the basketball on the floor. After the items were placed in the back, he opened the door for Brittany. Once inside he let out a huge breath.

"I haven't had fun like that in a long time," Brittany began.

I gave her my last breath.

"You really know how to take a girl on a first date. I would have never expected something like this. Thank you so much. I really enjoyed myself."

"You're welcome. I like to pride myself on being different and doing things out of the norm. Most guys like to do dinner and a movie. There's nothing wrong with that, but it's just too predictable. I like to keep you on your toes."

"That you did. When you said to wear jeans and sneakers I was like, huh? I've never worn jeans and sneakers on a first date. You did your thing, Mr. Montgomery."

"Are you hungry?"

"I could eat."

"What are you in the mood for?"

"After today, I'm in the mood for some good wings and a cold beer."

"That sounds good. Any spot in particular you like?"

"Have you ever been to J.R. Crickets?"

"Best lemon pepper wings on the planet."

"Is there one near here? I usually go to the one on Cascade."

"There's one in Smyrna. That's the one I go to all of the time."

Kevin pressed a button on his steering wheel. A voice came through the speakers.

"Good evening, Mr. Montgomery," a voice spoke. "How may I help you?"

"I need directions to J.R. Cricket's in Smyrna, Georgia."

"One moment please."

"I could have told you where it was," Brittany said.

"I know. I just wanted to show off."

The two laughed as the voice continued."

"I'm sending the directions to your navigational system. Is there anything else I can do for you?"

"That's all. Thank you."

"Enjoy the rest of your evening. Goodbye."

"I guess that's like OnStar for rich people," Brittany giggled.

"I pay for it. I might as well use it."

"True indeed."

3
Origins

The fun that Kevin and Brittany had that day led to a connection between them that was unexplainable. Through numerous phone conversations, text messages, Skype sessions and time together, the couple found that they had so much in common. They grew up in two different cities, but they were the same type of city. Kevin was from Fayetteville, NC and Brittany hailed from Florence, SC. With the exception of the military base in Fayetteville, it was a blue collar town just like Florence. The working class relied on employment from the local plants and factories.

They were both only children that came from two-parent homes and grew up in the suburbs. Even though their parents provided good lives for them they weren't spoiled and they did not get everything they wanted. Kevin's father worked at one of the local plants in Fayetteville and his mother was an elementary school teacher. That was the reason Kevin went to school for education. Brittany's father managed a restaurant and her mother worked in administration for a hospital.

Being only children, neither of them hung with a lot of people growing up. They had a small circle of friends that consisted of three to four people. Kevin entered the workforce at sixteen years old. His first job was at a grocery store. Because of all the after school clubs and cheerleading, Brittany didn't have the time to work a real job. She made her money doing hair and babysitting.

Throughout high school, Kevin worked and kept a low profile. He never cared about popularity, but because of his personality and ability to talk to people, a lot of people knew him. He was a smart student. In order for him to keep his job, he had to keep his grades up. He also knew that if he wanted to go to a school other than Fayetteville State, Methodist College or Fayetteville Tech, he had to keep his grades up so that he could earn a scholarship.

Hard work eventually paid off for Kevin. He received full academic scholarship offers from three prominent schools in North Carolina: North Carolina State, Wake Forest and The University of North Carolina at Chapel Hill. He always wanted to attend Duke University. He got accepted, but he couldn't afford it even with the partial scholarship that they offered. After a long decision process, Kevin chose NC State.

Brittany's road was slightly different. Until she got to high school, Brittany wore glasses and had braces. Because she was an only child, her father was very protective of her. At the time her braces came off and her vision corrected itself, she started to blossom into a young woman. Even with her newfound beauty she still kept to herself. In school, she became that mysterious, pretty girl that all the guys were curious about. She got good grades in school, but outside of her clubs and cheering, she really didn't have a life.

Her father didn't allow her to date until she was sixteen. The only thing she ever wore that boys could get a glance of her body in was her cheerleader's uniform.

When she did go on a date, he or her mother would take her and pick her up and there. Every boy she tried to date got frustrated quickly because they could never get her alone.

After high school she chose to go as far away from home as possible. She received a full scholarship to cheer at Clemson University. For the first time, Brittany was away from home and was no longer under the thumb of her father.
She...went...BUCK...WILD! Her first roommate, another girl on the cheerleading squad, helped her change her style and introduced her to the party life. Unlike other girls that went wild when they got to college, Brittany didn't sleep with every guy she met.

Needless to say, with her new lifestyle, she only lasted two years at Clemson. Her father was furious that she returned home as a college drop out. He turned her away. Brittany moved in with her grandmother until she saved enough money to move to Atlanta with a best friend from high school that was a student at Georgia Tech.

Kevin graduated in four years from NC State and returned to Fayetteville and took a job as an English teacher at his old high school. He loved teaching, but in his mind he felt that he was destined for so much more. During his fifth year, he bumped into a guy by the name of Derrick. Derrick was always considered a hustler. He always had something going on. He told him how much money he was making in real estate and how wide open the market was in Atlanta. He gave Kevin his card and told him that if he was ever interested and wanted a career change to give him a call.

During a trip to Atlanta he called Derrick. Derrick picked Kevin up from his hotel in a black Aston Martin and showed him the lifestyle he could now afford. The night included dinner at one of the most exclusive restaurants in Atlanta, VIP status at every club they went to and the icing on the cake was when Derrick took Kevin to his house.

After that weekend, Kevin returned to his one bedroom apartment in Fayetteville. As he looked around, it didn't take him long to realize that he wanted more. He finished the school year, packed up his apartment and moved to Atlanta.

Derrick took Kevin under his wing and stayed true to his word. For six months, Kevin never left his mentor's side. While completing the course to receive his real estate license, Derrick taught Kevin everything he knew about the business. The reason Derrick took him everywhere was because he wanted the people in the industry to get used to his face. That way when he stepped out on his own, the strength of Derrick's reputation would help him out when dealing with real estate agents, mortgage brokers and lenders.

For the remainder of his first year, Kevin did everything from locating properties to project managing. After that, Derrick felt like Kevin was finally ready to fly solo. With the help of one of Derrick's investors, Kevin successfully flipped his first house. Kevin cried the day he held his first check for $25,000 in his hand. Armed with all the tools he needed and Derrick's blessing, Kevin set out to start his own empire. In seven years he built a business that took him from renting a one bedroom apartment in Decatur and driving a 2001 Mitsubishi Galant to his current residence in Buckhead and owner of his three babies...all paid for.

Brittany, on the other hand, struggled when she got to Atlanta. Because she never received her degree, she had a hard time finding a job to pay her enough money to live comfortably on. She was okay until her best friend got engaged. This forced her to move out on her own. The only apartment she could find that she could afford that wasn't in a bad neighborhood was out in Cobb County. After she moved, her commute was horrible and for the money she was making, wasn't worth the drive.

She wound up quitting her job and became a bartender at a sports bar that was closer to her place. One slow, Monday night a young man came in and sat at the bar with a group of his friends, two other guys and three females. The guys were dressed in t-shirts, jeans, sneakers and hats. The ladies were scantily clad. The group was no trouble despite how loud they were. They treated Brittany very well. At the end of their meal, they paid and left. Brittany was disgusted because their bill was almost $500 and they didn't leave her a tip.

Five minutes later, the leader of the group walked back into the establishment. He introduced himself as J-Rock and gave Brittany five one hundred dollar bills. He went on to tell her that she could make that kind of money every night if she came to bartend for him at his club. Brittany took his number and called him the next day. She was hesitant when she found out his club was a strip club, but for that kind of money, she overlooked that part.

That Thursday night, Brittany started as the new bartender at Club Ebony. Her uniform consisted of a black, baby tee, that barely covered her chest, with the club's name on the front, shorts that revealed the bottom of her cheeks and black sneakers with black knee socks. At the time, she didn't know it, but J-Rock had plans for her.

Night after night, J-Rock would send dancers to make small talk with Brittany and flaunt their earnings, talk about the lives they live and the things that they buy. The night that decided it all for Brittany was when her car broke down and she asked XXXplosive, one of the dancers, to pick her up for work. She pulled up in Brittany's complex driving a silver, convertible Mercedes Benz SLK250. When she sat on the supple leather seats of the car, she looked at her Honda Civic sitting dead beside them. It was time for a change.

When she went in that night, she asked J-Rock to give her a shot at dancing. He calmly obliged her request, gave her the information she needed to obtain her dancers permit and sent her back to the bar. The process of getting her permit took a couple of days. While she waited for that, XXXplosive took her to a couple of spots where she could purchase her outfits and some shoes. Noticing how well a pair of earrings she wore matched her skin tone, XXXplosive gave Brittany the name of her alter ego. Sapphire was born.

4
Leap of Faith

On a warm April day, Kev and Rich stood in front of a foreclosed property in the Grant Park area of downtown Atlanta. The property was a three bedroom, one and a half bath, brick Ranch style home. The yard was overtaken by tall grass and weeds. The exterior didn't look that bad, but the inside was horrible. There were holes in the walls, floors and ceilings. The appliances were missing and the bathrooms were in shambles.

"What do you think?" Kevin asked Rich as he laughed.

"Are they all this bad in the beginning?"

"This is one of the better ones."

"I'd hate to see one of the worse ones," Rich replied.

"The first thing I want you to do is walk around and take pictures of the entire place, inside and out. You're going to have to have visual proof that it looked like this once the rehab is finished. People are never going to believe you once they see the final product."

Kevin walked through the house as Rich snapped pictures.

"Did the girl from Ruth Chris ever call you?"

"She didn't call. She came down to the shop the next day. Her date never showed up that night."

"Did you ask her out?"

"We went out for drinks that night and dinner the next night. We've pretty much been inseparable ever since. As a matter of fact, we're going to dinner tonight."

"What does she do?"

"She's a financial advisor with Morgan Stanley."

"Sounds like you two have a lot in common."

"Indeed we do. Do you know how refreshing it is to be able to sit down with a beautiful woman and talk money and the conversation is not about her trying to get yours?"

"I can only dream of that day."

"I've found my equal…mentally and financially. I think she might be the one."

"Slow your role, Speedy Gonzales. She sounds like an amazing person, but take your time."

"Did you mention anything to her about this venture?"

"I mentioned it, but I didn't go into great detail."

I gave her my last breath.

"Keep it that way for now. You also may want to look into getting a financial advisor of your own. Things are going to move forward and upward very quickly for you."

"Who do you use?"

"I'm with the Isley Firm. The CEO is one of my golf buddies. I can set you up if you like."

"I see where you're going. If she finds out that I don't have my own advisor, she's going to push to use her firm."

"Exactly. You and her may work out, but you don't want her hands on your finances. Feel me? One false move can cause a tremendous loss. You know how some females are."

"You're preaching to the choir, my brother."

"All jokes aside, though. I am happy for you. It sounds like you've found a good one."

"What about you? Any ladies on the horizon for you?"

"I have met someone. She's a little out of my norm, but there's something about her."

"What do you mean?"

"I met her at the bachelor party I went to about a month back."

"She's a stripper?"

"Yeah, but like I said, there's something different with her. She has goals that she is trying to fulfill. I believe that if she's true to what she says, I can help her."

"What is she trying to do?"

"She's in school to be an esthetician. She wants to open her own spa."

"That sounds like a good plan."

"If I can just convince her to stop dancing and focus on school, she can knock that out and be one step closer."

"How is she going to make money? Dancing is probably what's financing her dream right now."

"I was thinking about offering her a job. One of my colleagues is looking for an assistant. It won't be dancer money, but she'll be able to pay her bills and pay for school."

"All I can say is talk to her about it. See how she feels. If she really wants to stop dancing, she'll see this as an opportunity. If she's not serious, she'll give you every excuse in the book as to why she can't."

"You think so?"

"I know so. Just take the same advice you just gave me. Take your time."

"I knew I liked you for a reason," Kevin laughed.

"I'm a likable guy."

———————

Kevin and Rich wrapped up their conversation and business for the day. A week later, the property was purchased. Two weeks after that, the rehab began. Kevin split time between project managing, Rich's first flip and his own endeavors. Through it all, he managed to squeeze Brittany into his busy schedule. It would make things so much better if she had a normal schedule. Kevin felt it was time to see if Brittany was really willing to achieve her goals.

If Kevin and Brittany weren't able to see each other during the week, Sunday was the one day they could always count on. That afternoon they decided to spend a quiet day at Kevin's place. Brittany was soaking in the Jacuzzi as Kevin stood at the grill engulfed in a cloud of smoke preparing their dinner for the evening.

Once the meal was completed and served, Kevin

called to Brittany. She climbed out of the Jacuzzi. Kevin watched as the water ran down her flesh as she exited the hot tub. Brittany toweled herself off then wrapped the towel around her waist leaving her red, bikini topped, B cups exposed.

"This looks absolutely amazing," she complimented as she sat down.

"I'm glad it is to your liking."

"I've always been a sucker for a man that can cook."

"What would you like to drink?"

"Since this is chicken and shrimp, what do you have in a white?"

"I have Riesling, Chardonnay and a nice Sauvignon Blanc."

"Let's go with the Sauvignon Blanc."

"Excellent choice, Mademoiselle."

Kevin uncorked the bottle of wine, poured two glasses then took his seat. He grabbed his fork and stabbed into his salad. Brittany popped him on the hand.

"Not before we say grace," she scolded.

"I'm sorry. I lost my head for a moment."

The couple grabbed hands as Kevin blessed their meal.

"Dear Lord, we thank you for this meal that we are about to receive. May it nourish our bodies as you nourish our minds and spirit. We are thankful for the many blessings that you have given us, but I'm most thankful for the blessing of this amazing woman that you have allowed to come into my life. Amen."

"Amen. That was beautiful."

"Thank you."

The two begin to eat their meals as they engaged in small talk. About ten minutes into the meal, Kevin felt it was time to talk about something of a more serious nature.

"I want to talk to you about something serious if you don't mind."

"Okay…what's on your mind?"

"I've noticed that over these past couple of weeks, you've had nothing but ill words to speak of the club."

"I'm at my wits end with that place but I have to do what I have to do."

"If there was an alternative route, would you be willing to take it?"

"Depending on what it was."

"I believe I have a way for you to stop dancing so that you can go to school full-time."

"Before we go any further, is this conversation because you want me to stop dancing or are you really interested in my future."

"A little of the first part, a lot of the second part. I met you in the club. It bothers me a little that you dance but not enough for me to let you go. I love watching you when you talk about finishing school and opening your own spa. Your eyes light up and I can hear the passion in your voice. That shows me how much you really want it."

"That has been my goal and dream since I moved to Atlanta. I didn't graduate from college, but I'm still determined to be successful in my own right."

"I believe that you can do anything you set your mind to.

I gave her my last breath.

That's what attracts me to you the most."

"Now that I know how you really feel, what did you have in mind?"

"Do you remember Selena, from my office?"

"The lady I met at the barbeque we went to a week or so after we met."

"Yes. Selena is looking for an executive assistant. I told her about you and she said she would like to sit down and talk to you."

"What kind of money is she offering?"

"I'll put it like this…it's not what you would make as a dancer, but you will be able to pay for your living expenses and your tuition. She also said that she would work around your school schedule. This is something you can do from home. You may have to come into the office a couple times a week tops."

"That sounds very interesting."

"This is the opportunity for you to finally have a normal schedule and stop living those vampire hours."

"It'll take some getting used to, but I think I can manage."

"I know that the summer session is coming up and she also agreed to give you an advance so that you can pay your tuition, fees and get the things you need for school. She'll just deduct it from your pay a little at a time."

"You did all of this for me?"

"A good man is supposed to have his woman's back and support her in all that she wants to do."

"Can I sleep on it?"

"I need an answer now. If I don't call her this evening, she's going to hire someone else tomorrow."

Brittany paused for a moment and gave it some thought. While thinking, she swirled her fork around in her pasta salad. Kevin continued to eat.

"I'll do it."

"You will?"

"Yes. Its time I step out and take that leap of faith. You believe in me or you wouldn't have gone through all of this trouble. Its time I believe in myself."

"That's great. I'll give Selena a call as soon as we finish eating."

"Call her now."

Kevin pulled his cell phone out of his pocket and went to his contacts to find Selena's number. Once he found it, he called. Brittany sat on edge as she listened to one side of the conversation. Three minutes later, the conversation was over.

"What did she say?"

"She said to meet her at Copeland's on Cobb Parkway tomorrow at one o'clock."

"Tomorrow? That's no good. I don't have anything to wear."

"Come on."

Kevin grabbed Brittany's hand and led her into the house and into his bedroom. He sat her in the black leather armchair that he had in his room.

"Close your eyes. No peeking." He walked into his closet and pulled out a black suit bag. He laid the bag across Brittany's lap. "Okay…you can open them now."

Brittany opened her eyes.

"What is this?"

"I know you have tons of clothes, but I didn't know whether or not you had any business clothes. I knew you would need something for your interview and I knew that if you didn't have anything to wear, you may not have had time to go get something. Open it up."

Brittany unzipped the bag to reveal a navy blue business suit and white blouse.

"Is this Dolce & Gabanna?"

"I want you to get a taste of what success is going to bring you." As she was admiring the suit, he reached under his bed and pulled out a shoe box that was in a Neiman Marcus bag, "No outfit is complete without shoes."

Like a kid on Christmas, Brittany tore into the bag. When she saw the name on the box, her eyes lit up.

"Are these what I think they are?"

"Christian Louboutin…or as the average ratchet would say…the red bottoms." Kevin laughed.

"I really don't know what to say."

"You don't have to say anything. This is just a small gesture from me to you. I enjoy the finer things in life and as the woman in my life, you should, too."

Brittany placed the box with the shoes in them on the floor beside the chair and stood up. She carefully draped the hanging bag over the back of the chair. Brittany dropped the towel that was wrapped around her bottom half and slowly walked toward Kevin.

When she arrived to him she pressed her body against his and wrapped her arms around his neck and pulled his lips to hers. While kissing him deeply and passionately, she pushed him from the foot of the bed around to the side of the bed then pushed him onto it.

Kevin slid back as she crawled on top of him. Brittany worked her hands under his shirt, sliding it up his body then off. He lay bare-chested as she straddled his waist. Brittany reached behind her back and pulled the string of her bikini top to expose her perky breasts. She moaned as she rubbed her own nipples and looked down at her man. She laid her naked chest on his as she once again kissed him deeply.

From his lips she moved to his neck. With her tongue, she followed the path between his muscular pecks. She moved further down that path kissing each ab on the way to his waist. With her teeth, and a little help from Kevin, Brittany peeled his basketball shorts off. She did the same with the Calvin Klein boxer briefs he wore.

Once her man was completely naked, she took his sword in her hand and slowly stroked it up and down. She let out a devilish giggle then gave Kevin an evil grin before she swallowed half of his erect manhood. With one hand she stroked him as she devoured his dick. With the other she made sure his two attached friends weren't left out of the fun. Every man tries to maintain his cool when he is getting head, but when it's that good, he can't control it. Kevin released moans of ecstasy as he was being pleasured.

Being the giving man that he was, Kevin couldn't allow her to have all of the fun. He pushed her back and stood her up. With the strength of his muscular arms, he turned Brittany's 5'5" frame upside down putting her freshly shaven pussy in licking distance. He pleasured her as she did the same to him. After about fifteen minutes, he put her down but only for a brief second. Kevin lifted Brittany back into the air and then pulled her body close to him. He then positioned his arms in the

I gave her my last breath.

bend of her knees and lowered her
down toward his lower body.
Brittany reached behind herself
once again. This time it was to
grab his dick so that she could
position it to slide inside of her as
he lowered her down.

"Kevin!" Brittany screamed
as his hard and thick love muscle
entered her wet, yet tight, tunnel of
love.

Up and down she bounced,
biting her bottom lip and moaning
with every stroke. This position
went on for a good five minutes.
When he couldn't hold her up any
longer, he threw her to the bed.
Still on her back, Kevin climbed
on the bed and re-entered her. With
slow, long strokes he played a
crucial game of tag with her G-
spot.

Kevin and Brittany's sexual
excursion lasted for about an hour
and a half. They explored each
other's bodies in every way and

position possible. Once they were spent, they laid breathless in the middle of the bed. Brittany rested her head on his chest and listened to Kevin's heartbeat.

"You know," Brittany began as she brushed the hair out of her face. "For the first time, in a long time, I really feel that I've found a man that is into me for who I am, not what I do."

"I never thought in a million years that I would ever ask a dancer out, but there was just something about you. I don't frequent strip clubs, but I've been to a few. The way you talked to me and treated me the night we met showed me that you were more than just a dancer. The more time we spend together the more your inner beauty shines through."

"To be honest, I've never dated anyone I've met at the club. I've had plenty of offers, but I just couldn't allow myself to do it. The guys that come in are looking for a fantasy. In my world, I tried to remain that fantasy that a man would love to have, but it's unobtainable. It was never about meeting men. It has always been about making money."

"Are you sure that leaving that world is something you're ready to do?"

"Yes. Even before I met you, I was searching for a way to get out of that life. After seven years, it was really starting to take a negative toll on me."

"How so?"

"I've done everything in my power not to get caught up in the drug and alcohol abuse. Lately, everywhere I turn its right there."

"It seems like I came along at the right time."

"Yes, you did. I really appreciate everything you've done and are doing for me. I mean that from the heart."

"Before I met you, it has been all business all of the time. You've come into my life and allowed me to see that life is about more than just business and making money. Like the old saying goes, success is nothing if you don't have anyone special to share it with."

"I'm not successful yet, but when I get there, I hope you're still there to share it with me."

"I'm not going anywhere."

"Do you promise?"

"I promise."

5
Shaky Ground

That Saturday night in June was warm. The air was crisp and fresh. Under the lights in Kevin's backyard, Melissa, Brittany, Kevin and Rich gathered to celebrate the success of Rich's first house flip. Dressed in casual wear the ladies sat sipping wine as the men enjoyed fine cognac. Dinner ended and they sat in lounge chairs by the pool. Brittany draped herself over Kevin. Melissa sat in her own chair as Rich sat in his.

"Has it set in yet?" Kevin asked Rich as he took a sip of his drink.

"I must've looked at that check a hundred times today."

"Hopefully that will be the first of many."

"That's what I'm hoping for."

"What are you going to do with the money?" Brittany inquired. "If you don't mind me asking."

"I haven't decided yet."

"My mentor told me that after every flip, I should buy myself something nice or either take a trip. I still do that to this day."

"That sounds like good advice. I have been thinking about redoing my basement and turning it into my man cave."

"Well, there you go."

"I think you should invest it," Melissa interjected. "That money can make you a lot more if you do it right."

"I have an appointment with my financial advisor on Monday. He and I have to sit down and talk about a few things."

"You never told me you had a financial advisor."

"Kevin introduced me to his guy at the Isley Firm."

"The Isley Firm? Why not Morgan Stanley."

"After doing my research of both firms, I just felt like The Isley Firm was better for me. Besides, I like to support black-owned businesses."

Melissa folded her arms and turned up her nose. Rich got up, sat beside Melissa and wrapped his arms around her.

"It's nothing against you or your firm. This was just a personal preference."

Kevin felt like he needed to lighten the mood.

"Speaking of personal preference, my company is taking our annual trip to Vegas next month. We'll be there for a week. You two are welcome to come along."

"I just started working with Selena. I don't know if I can take that kind of time off yet."

"Baby, Selena is a part of my company. She's going, too."

"In that case, Vegas here we come!"

"What about you, Melissa?" Rich asked. "Can your firm spare you for a week?"

"I don't know. I'll have to see if my schedule will permit."

Kevin stood up and raised his glass.

"Ladies and gentleman," he laughed as he began, "last year was a rough year for me. I had some setbacks and some failures, but I continued to press on. I promised myself that 2015 would be so much better. We're halfway through the year and I've made leaps and bounds in real estate. I've gained a friend that I am now proud to call a business associate. Last but not least, I've found a smart, determined and beautiful woman. This year has started off with a bang for me. To 2015!"

"To 2015!" The rest spoke simultaneously.

The night went on and before long, Rich and Melissa were gone. Kevin sat on the couch. Brittany was curled up beside him with her head in his lap.

"Can you turn that down for a minute?" Brittany requested. Kevin lowered the volume on the television. "Did you notice how Melissa was acting toward Rich tonight?"

"She's just a little upset that he didn't choose an advisor at her firm."

"I know that, but I'm talking about the entire night. Every time he tried to show her affection, she pulled away."

"Maybe she's not into public displays of affection like we are."

"Didn't you say they met around the same time we did?"

"They met the night before I met you."

"I'm just saying. That's a long time to be dealing with someone and still act like he's a stranger to you. She just seems so cold and distant."

"Rich doesn't seem to have a problem with it."

"Rich is a good guy. He's spiritual and he embraces his blackness and his heritage. I've never seen a corporate woman with that kind of guy."

"Rich is also well off. He has a Bachelor's in Marketing and he also has an MBA."

"Really? I never knew that."

"I've seen Melissa's type before. It's like she doesn't know how to separate her two worlds."

"What do you mean?"

"There's corporate Melissa and there's private Melissa. In corporate America, there is a certain standard that you have to abide by and live up to in public."

"But she was among friends tonight."

"I don't think she considers us as friends just yet. This is her first time being around us in an intimate setting. Give her time. She'll come around."

"I hope she does because Rich is a good one. She'd be a fool to let him get away. I know plenty of girls looking for a guy like Rich."

"You just keep Cinnamon, Vixen and Bootylicious away from my boy. He has a woman."

"I have friends that aren't dancers."

"Name one." Brittany paused for a minute. "Exactly." Kevin laughed.

"You know what? That's a damn shame. I don't have any normal friends."

"We gravitate to the people we're around the most. That's understandable."

"It's still a damn shame."

The weekend ended and the work week began. Since Rich's project was over, Kevin had a light day. After leaving a meeting with a lender that morning in Buckhead, he decided to stop by Rich's shop to have his Camaro detailed. We he pulled up and parked. He noticed Melissa walking out of the building with a scowl on her face. Kevin spoke to her, but she ignored him as she got in her BMW and sped off.

Kevin entered the building and asked for Rich. The receptionist showed him to his office. Kevin knocked on the door. When Rich commanded him to enter, he noticed that he was sitting behind his desk staring at the computer screen.

"You alright? I just saw Melissa leaving."

"I'm good. She's still upset about me not choosing her firm. She'll get over it. What's up with you, my brother?"

"I was in the area and decided to bring the Camaro down and get her cleaned up."

"What color is it?"

"Silver."

Rich pressed the intercom button on his phone.

"Yes Rich?" The receptionist's voice answered.

"Have Lonnie take the silver Camaro outside and give it the works."

"The platinum package?"

"Yes."

"Will do."

"I appreciate that."

"It's the least I can do."

"Can I ask you something personal?"

"What's up?"

"Are things really okay with you and Melissa? The only reason I ask is because I noticed that she was a little cold and distant the other night."

"Last week was a shaky week for us, but all in all, we're good. Every relationship has its ups and downs. Besides, Melissa isn't one for displaying affection in public like I am. That's a work in progress."

"That's the same thing I told my girl."

"She's used to being with the stuffed suit corporate type guys. I can roll with the best of them. I'm just in a different package."

"I can feel that. As long as you're okay."

"Once this whole thing blows over, we'll be back to

normal. I appreciate the concern though. Like I told you, I don't deal with too many guys down here. You've always shot me straight and kept it one hundred with me."

"That's all I know. I'll always have your back, homie."

"And I yours."

Kevin and Rich continued to talk while Kevin waited for his car detailing to be finished. Once he it was done, he headed to the office to see what he had to do for the rest of the week. When he arrived, Selena was waiting for him.

Selena was a Hispanic woman in her early forties from New Jersey. She was around 5'7" with that light, Puerto Rican skin tone. Her hair hung curly and her eyes were coffee brown. After brokering Kevin's first flip, they built a business relationship. A year after that, she became his in-house broker and an investor.

She was a real estate powerhouse with fifteen years of experience. Every major real estate firm and agent came to Selena when they needed a broker. A few of her connections were the reason that Kevin became so successful as quickly as he did.

"May I speak to you for a minute, Kevin?"

"Step into my office. I'll be there as soon as I get my messages."

Selena walked into Kevin's office and sat down in one of the leather armed chairs in front of his desk. Kevin was right behind her. He took his place behind his desk."

"What's going on?"

"This is about Brittany."

"Is something wrong?"

"Everything has been great up until a week ago. I haven't been able to get her on the phone. When she returns my calls, its hours later. On the days that she was supposed to come into the office, she's late. I don't know what's going on with her. She does a great job for me. That is why I'm concerned."

"I was so tied up with Rich's closing last week, I hadn't noticed any change in her routine. I'll speak to her tonight."

"It's not that big of a deal. I just wanted to make sure everything is okay with her. If she has some things to take care off, I'm sure we can work something out. Let her know that I'm not angry. I just want to make sure she is okay."

"I'll let you know as soon as I find out what's going on."

"Thank you, Kevin."

Selena left as Kevin pondered about what could be going on in Brittany's life that he didn't know about. He shook it off and continued his business for the day.

Later on that night, he called Brittany, but there was no answer. He sent her a text and the response said that she was tied up and couldn't talk. This went on for a couple of days. Kevin finally got fed up and went to her place that Thursday night. She wasn't home. Where could she be? Kevin remembered her saying that she had been hanging out with one of the girls from the club lately. From her house, Kevin drove to Club Ebony. Sure enough, she was there…in full dancer gear.

Not wanting to make a scene, Kevin sat at the bar. Brittany didn't know he was there until she got on the main stage. A streak of fear shot through her body, but she maintained while she was on stage. After her songs, she shyly walked over to Kevin like she was a child that had just been caught doing wrong.

"What are you doing here, Baby?" Brittany asked hesitantly.

"I was getting ready to ask you the same thing."

"Don't be mad. I have a reasonable explanation, but now isn't a good time."

"How long have you been lying to me about this?"

"I swear…I've only been back here since last week."

The manager of the club, J-Rock noticed the conversation between Brittany and Kevin and walked over. J-Rock was about 5'7" with dark brown skin and cornrows.

"Is there a problem, Sapphire?"

"Everything is cool, J-Rock."

"Everything is not cool," Kevin interrupted. "Go get your things, we're leaving."

"She ain't goin' nowhere until she pay me back the money she owe me."

"What money?"

"She owes me two stacks."

"For what?"

"J-Rock loaned me the money to get my car fixed right before I met you. I was paying him back a little at a time."

Kevin reached in his back pocket and pulled out his checkbook.

"Who do I make this out to?"

"Sorry homeboy…cash only."

"I don't carry that kind of cash on me. I'll have it for you tomorrow night."

"No problem. I'll see you tomorrow. You have a pleasant evening." J-Rock smirked and walked away.

"Get your things. We're leaving."

"Okay."

Brittany walked away with the saddest look on her face. She went to the dressing room. Ten minutes later she returned pulling her bag behind her. Because she'd caught a ride to work with one of the other dancers, she had to ride home with Kevin. That was the quietest ride she ever had to endure. Nothing was said until they pulled up in front of Brittany's apartment.

"Please don't be mad, Baby," Brittany pleaded.

"Mad…no. Disappointed…very."

"Understand it from my point of view. You've done so much for me to this point. I couldn't come to you with this one. This happened before we met."

"Maybe I would feel better if you had just been straight up with me. I had no clue what was

116

going on until Selena said something to me a few days ago."

"What did Selena say?"

"She said that everything was good until last week. You've been late; she hasn't been able to get in touch with you."

"I'm sorry. I thought I could handle the job, school and dancing a few nights a week to pay off my debt."

"You know I would do anything in the world for you. All you have to do is come to me. I'm your man. That's what I'm supposed to do."

"I know, Baby. It's just that...I've never had a man have my back like you do. This is taking some getting used to. I promise you it will never happen again."

"I don't like being lied to or deceived."

Kevin turned his head and stared out of the window.

"I'll make it up to you. I promise."

"We're cool."

"Do you want to come in?"

"I just need to be alone right now so I can calm down. I'll call you later."

Brittany kissed Kevin on the cheek and got out of the car. Once she was safely inside her apartment. Kevin drove off. He rode in silence to his place. Once he arrived he walked into his backyard, sat down by the pool and gazed at the stars as if searching for answers. Two hours later he went in and retired for the night.

The next morning, Kevin woke up feeling better than the night before. He took what Brittany told him to heart and realized that people are going to make mistakes. Given the extreme lifestyle change Brittany had to undergo, he felt that there was no need to hold a grudge or try to punish her for it.

Later on that night, Kevin arrived at Club Ebony to pay off Brittany's debt. The club had just opened so it was empty. The girl at the door escorted Kevin to J-Rock's office. J-Rock was sitting behind his desk going over some paperwork.

"What's up?" J-Rock greeted. "Have a seat."

Kevin took a seat in front of the desk, reached into his inside jacket pocket and tossed a banded stack of one hundred dollar bills on the desk.

"This should cover Brittany's debt."

"Can I speak at you for a minute, man to man?"

"What's on your mind?"

"I've been in this business a long time and I've seen a lot of things. This whole situation with you taking Sapphire out of the club, I get it. I always knew she was different and dancing wasn't her whole life. I know she has dreams just like every other chick that comes through here."

"Get to your point."

"I see you with ya Maserati and ya custom suits and I respect ya hustle. The point I'm trying to make is that when these women enter this life, no matter what intentions they have, their mindset always changes. When it comes to men, it's all about seeing how much they can get out of them. They say and do anything they can to get exactly what they want. You seem like you're set as far as cash is concerned so you don't have to worry about her tapping you out, but once she feels she's gotten everything she possibly can, she'll be on to the next. For your sake and hers, I hope I'm wrong, but I seldom am."

Kevin stood up and straightened his jacket. He grinned at J-Rock then walked out of his office. Although he didn't let on while sitting in front of him, J-Rock's words sunk in deep. Kevin had never dealt with type of woman like Brittany. He wasn't stone to her, but he was somewhat guarded.

6
Buckled Down

The aftermath of incident
between Kevin and Brittany wasn't
as bad as it could've been. Kevin
had to check Brittany to really see
where her loyalty was. The things
he had done for her were no small
feats. Paying the debt was nothing
to him. He's blown more money
on things with no purpose. It was
the principle behind it. Kevin was
trying to show Brittany that he was
there for her no matter what.
Brittany had never dealt with a guy
like Kevin who gave unselfishly
with no concealed motive. She
knew that if she wanted to keep
him in her life, she had to show
and prove.

For two weeks following the confrontation at the club, Kevin kept Brittany at a distance. He called to check on her from time to time but carried on with business as usual. This was the first time Brittany wasn't receiving the attention that she was used to from him and it drove her crazy. For those two weeks she felt like the girl she was in high school. The only thing she knew to do was to show him that she was serious. Brittany became a model employee at work and one of the top students in her class.

Kevin and Brittany were seldom at the office at the same time. One Friday afternoon, she pulled up and saw his Camaro parked outside. She got excited due to the fact that she hadn't seen him face to face in almost a week. Brittany pulled her visor down and checked her hair and makeup in the mirror. She grabbed her briefcase and walked into the office. Selena hadn't arrived yet, so she decided to drop in on Kevin. She lightly knocked on the door.

"Yes," Kevin commanded.

Brittany poked her head in the door.

"Hey…you got a minute?"

"Sure…come on in."

She walked in and sat down in one of the leather armchairs in front of Kevin's desk.

"How you doing?"

"I'm good," Kevin replied without looking away from his computer screen.

"Are you doing anything this weekend?"

"I don't have anything planned. Why? What's up?"

"I thought maybe we could spend some time together. It's been awhile."

"We'll see."

Kevin's tone began to frustrate Brittany.

"Okay…Kevin. I get it. I messed up, but you can't keep treating me like this. Kevin, look at me."

Kevin turned away from his computer monitor and looked into Brittany's eyes.

"I'm sorry. How many times do I have to apologize to you?"

"As many times as it takes for you to realize that I'm not some chump on the streets that you can lie to or keep secrets from. I've been straight up and honest with you from day one. It may not mean anything to you, but the truth means something to me. I know what kind of life you've lived. I know what kind of men you've dealt with and you know the type of females I've dealt with. I show you that I'm different, but still you treat me the same way you treated them. Everything I've done for you is because I care about you. I want to see you succeed. You told me your dreams and I've done what I can to help put you on the road to achieving them. There's so much more to come, but I have to know that you're down for me like I'm down for you. Can you understand that?"

Brittany sat back in the chair and exhaled. No man has ever put her in her place like that. She stood up and walked behind the desk. She swiveled him around to face her and sat on his lap.

"I'm so sorry, Baby. I didn't realize it was that serious. I didn't want to stress you with it. I honestly thought I could get the debt paid off and be done with it in a couple of weeks."

"I can feel that, but you should have come to me."

"I didn't look at it like that. That was a debt that I acquired before I met you."

"It doesn't matter. I'm with you now. You started school before I met you. You had your dreams before I met you."

"You're right. I promise you it'll never happen again."

"Just show me."

Brittany wrapped her arms around Kevin's neck and kissed him on the lips.

"You're not getting off that easy. A new institution has acquired your debt. We need to discuss repayment."

"Oh really?"

Brittany began to unbutton her blouse as somebody knocked on the door. Brittany jumped up and buttoned her blouse back up.

"Just a minute," Kevin called. Brittany continued to straighten her clothes then sat down in the chair she was sitting in. "Come in."

"There you are," Selena began as she walked into the

office. "I'm ready whenever you are, Brittany."

"I'll be there in just a second."

Selena paused for a second.

"Why do the two of you look guilty?"

"I'm grown," Kevin responded as he laughed.

"Uh huh," Selena giggled. "I'll be in my office."

Brittany got up to walk out behind her.

"I'll see you tonight. Come to the house when you finish up with Selena."

"Okay."

———————————

Three months passed. Brittany was halfway finished with school. Everything between her and Kevin was smooth. Rich was in the final stages of his second flip. During this time, Kevin prepared Brittany for life after school. Her entire mentality had changed. She no longer associated with anyone from the club. Through networking events and school, Brittany had a new circle of friends. These women were the type of women that she needed in her life. They were investors, business owners and other women with plans that they were implementing.

One particular woman took a strong liking to Brittany. Her name was Sybil Cannon. Sybil was from Miami and had a similar background to Brittany. She danced her way through cosmetology school. Once she was out of school, she opened her own salon. With constant networking, good business and a quality product, she closed her small shop and opened an exclusive salon in South Beach. This salon serviced the wives, girlfriends and side pieces of all of the athletes, entertainers along with most of the other powerful women of Miami. Her reputation eventually opened doors for her to open salons in Atlanta, New York and Los Angeles.

The same way Derrick took Kevin under his wing, Sybil did the same for Brittany. Beauty school taught Brittany the skills that she needed to know to provide the necessary service. Sybil taught her the business end of it. Brittany took full advantage of the people in her network. Any questions that she had, there was someone that could give her an answer.

Fall was on the horizon, but the weather was still hot in Atlanta. A warm Saturday afternoon found Kevin and Brittany walking into Kevin's place after a day of shopping at Lenox Mall and Phipps Plaza. Brittany still had her place, but she spent most of her time and nights at Kevin's. He combined his business attire and casual wear in order to give Brittany her own closet. Brittany put her bags in the closet, grabbed her laptop and joined Kevin in his man cave.

Brittany and Kevin were in the stage of their relationship where they didn't have to be up under each other when they were alone. They went on about their individual routines as they would if they were each in their own place. While Kevin watched Sports Center, Brittany curled up on the other end of the couch and opened her laptop.

"I've noticed you've been on your laptop a lot lately," Kevin observed. "What are you working on?"

"I'm working on my business plan."

"Really?"

"I'll be finished with school in about three more months. I don't want to waste any time. Sybil says that procrastination is not a good quality to have in our industry."

"That's true for any industry."

"I plan to make full use of the connections that I'm making and have made. It would be nice to be able to open my own spa right out of school."

"If you put the work in, it can happen."

"Do you have a name for it?"

"The Sanctuary."

"That's catchy. I like it."

"Women call their bathrooms their sanctuary. When they take hot bubble baths with candles and wine, they feel at peace. That is how I want them to feel when they come into my place."

"Have you spoken with any potential investors?"

"Sybil is going to invest in it, but I don't want to approach anyone else until my business plan is done. I want all of their questions to have an answer right in front of them. Why? Do you want to invest in it?"

"Honestly, that's not my thing…it's a little too risky for me."

"And real estate isn't risky?"

"Real estate is what I know," Kevin laughed. "I'm not saying that it can't and won't be successful, I'm just more comfortable investing in something that has a larger payout."

"I can respect that."

"What I can do for you is help you find a building in a prime location at a good price. I also have the people in my network to do everything in it that you want done to it."

"I already have you down for that."

"Since when?"

"Since we first met. You told me that when I was ready, you could help me with that."

"You don't forget anything, do you?"

"Nope."

"Hypothetically speaking...let's say we break up tomorrow. Would you still help me?"

"Hypothetically...yes. In real life...no."

"That's cold," Brittany laughed as she threw a pillow at him.

"Well...you don't have to worry about that because I'm not going anywhere and neither are you."

Monday afternoon, Kevin met Rich at a Jamaican spot for lunch in downtown Atlanta. When Kevin walked in, Rich stood up to greet his friend and business associate. The smile on Rich's face disappeared when he noticed what Kevin was wearing.

"My brother," Rich greeted with absolute sincerity. "Is everything okay?"

"I'm fine. Why do you ask?"

"It's a work day and you have on jeans."

"Are you serious?" Kevin laughed.

"The only time I've seen you out of a suit during the week is when we play ball."

"I'm trying something different. My girl said I should try to loosen up a little. I don't have to meet with any clients today, so I decided to make it casual Monday."

"I'm just checking. I thought you were sick or something."

"Anyway…what's good with you?"

"Everything…the sun is shining, I'm healthy and so is my bank account."

"Hopefully by Friday that account will be a lot healthier."

"Are we set to close Friday?"

"That's the plan. The investor did his final walkthrough last Monday, the inspection and the appraisal was on my desk on Wednesday and we approved his offer that same afternoon. He moved the money into escrow on Friday. The only reason why we couldn't close today is because he is coming in town on Thursday and wants to do the closing in person. That's just his thing."

"It sounds like you've been working hard."

"I don't play around when it comes to making money."

"I see that."

"Now that business is out of the way, what's going on with you? How are things with you and Melissa?"

"Things couldn't be better. I believe the trip to Vegas was really what we needed. Since we've been back, she's been more receptive and has opened up to me a lot more."

"That's good to hear. I was worried about you for a minute."

"Worried about me? Why?"

"Speaking as an outsider looking into your relationship, things seemed one-sided."

"Honestly, it *was* like that for a while. I believe I was more into her than she was into me. I never told you, but I almost let her go and just couldn't do it. The challenge had me hooked. I felt that we had too much in common not to be compatible with each other."

"Does she know you did time?"

"I told her about that the first night we talked. I'm always open about that. It helped mold me into who I am."

"That's true. She overlooked that because you're successful. You know how her type can be. Had you just been the bus boy at Ruth Chris that night, she wouldn't have given you the time of day."

"Money changes a lot of things. I like our situation because it's not about the money, but because of it, she sees me as an equal and not a liability."

"That's real talk. It's the same way with me and Brittany. The things I do for her she can do for herself. I buy her nice things because that's what I like to do and not because I'm trying to be flashy. If I step out in an Armani suit, my lady should be laced in nothing less than Chanel and Prada."

"That's where you and I differ. I can afford those things, but it's not me..."

"Says the man who drives the Porsche," Kevin interrupted.

"The car is a different story all together. When I first started out, I could only afford hoopties and buckets. When I bought a car, it was so raggedy that I started saving for the next one because I didn't know how long it was going to last. I deserve my Porsche."

"The way I see it, I can't take it with me. I make enough to live the lifestyle I want to live. My parents are taken care of and I have plenty of money tucked away."

"But that's what I like about you. Money has changed your lifestyle, but it hasn't changed you. I've met so many brothers

I gave her my last breath.

that have started from the bottom
and as soon as they get to the top,
they slam the door shut. You didn't
have to do what you did for me.
You didn't know me from Adam."

"I learned that by watching
my father. He didn't have much,
but as long as his family was taken
care of, he was willing to help
anybody that he could and never
asked for a thing in return."

"It's a little bit different for
me. All the time I spent locked up,
I had nothing. I had to depend on
others to put money on my books.
Now that I have everything that I
could ever want, I hold on to it. I
help the ones that help me, but I'm
a little more frugal than the
average success story."

"I am friends with this guy,
if he walked in here right now, you
wouldn't know that his net worth
was around 45 million. He's the
stingiest, cheapest man I know. He
would always tell me that rich men

don't stay rich by giving or throwing their money away."

"That's a true statement. When you work hard for your money, you respect it more. Look at all these broke multi-million dollar lottery winners you hear about. My question to you is…do you give back to the community?"

"Without a doubt. I have a non-profit that does a number of things here in Atlanta and back in my hometown. In Atlanta my biggest project is called *Silver Meals*. We make sure that our seniors that can't afford groceries get three hot meals a day. It's geared toward African Americans, but anyone that needs help can get it."

"I see those trucks around the city all of time. I didn't know that was you."

"Every year I sponsor a Pop Warner football team and at the beginning of every school year

I partner with a few barber shops and we do back to school cuts and hand out backpacks full of supplies."

"I had no idea. You are truly a generous brother."

"I never knew what it was like to go without, but I've always had friends that did. I always said if I was ever in a position to help, I would. What about you?"

"I do a lot of speaking engagements at schools telling my story. I also donate heavily to the Boys and Girls Clubs. I said that one day I wanted to start a non-profit that help men and women that are fresh out of jail or prison to turn their lives around and not become a product of the system. I don't really know how to get it off the ground."

Kevin picked his phone up off of the table and began to scroll through numbers.

"Put this number in your phone: 404-555-7619. Her name is Dorothy Newton. She is the lady that helped me put my non-profit together. Give her a call and tell her that I gave you her number. She'll be able to help you with everything you need."

"Who don't you have in your network?" Rich chuckled as he put the number in his phone.

"In my line of work I meet all kinds of people. You'd be surprised how far a friendly conversation can take you."

The men continued to talk and eat. After the business lunch concluded, Kevin headed to the office. When he arrived, there was a gorgeous woman sitting in the waiting area. She looked to be in her mid to late thirties with a cocoa complexion. Her black, silky hair was pulled up into a bun. She stood up to greet Kevin when he arrived. The navy blue business suit hugged the contour of her hourglass figure. The top two buttons of her blouse allowing the cleavage of her D cups to peek out.

"Hello," Kevin greeted. "May I help you?"

"I'm waiting for Mr. Montgomery."

"I am he, but you can call me Kevin."

"It is a pleasure to finally meet you. Brittany talks about you nonstop. I'm Sybil."

"The infamous Sybil," Kevin extended his hand. "The pleasure is all mine. Please…step into my office."

Kevin led the way to his office then assumed his position behind his desk as Sybil sat down in one of the chairs in front of Kevin's desk.

"I'm sorry for stopping by without out an appointment. I hope I didn't catch you at a bad time."

"You actually caught me on a slow day. What can I do for you?"

"Brittany tells me you are the person to talk to when it comes to real estate."

"That depends on what your need is."

"Well…I'm based out of Miami, but because of some issues here in Atlanta with one of my businesses, I'm looking for a place here. I'm tired of living in hotels when I come to town."

"Is this temporary or would you like for this to be a permanent residence?"

"That's hard to say. On this trip I've been here for three months and I'll probably be here for another three then it's off to New York and LA to check on the shops there, then back to Miami. I come here the most though. I know I'll be here at least three to four months out of the year."

"Okay…I have a few options for you. I have an investor that has a couple of executive rental properties."

"Executive properties?"

"Yes…one is a townhouse and one is a condo. The townhouse is located in Vinings and the condo is in Atlantic Station. I'm not sure how familiar you are with the city."

"I know where Atlantic Station is, but I have no idea where Vinings is."

"Vinings is close to Buckhead. It's an upper class suburban area…very nice."

"You still haven't told me exactly what an executive property is."

"These are fully furnished places that are rented out to people like yourself that have to be here longer than you would like to have to live in a hotel room. The only drawback is that when you plan to come, they could possibly be occupied unless the investor knows exactly when you're coming."

"I never know when exactly I'm coming to town or leaving once I get here. I was only supposed to be here for a week and I'm in my third month. What else do you have?"

"I can check with my investment groups and other people within my network to see if someone has a property for sale. The thing with that is they sell for market price and I don't know if you want to take on another mortgage like that."

"Money is not an issue. I have wanted to buy another home somewhere, but I was thinking more of LA or New York."

"I saved this option for last because being a business man, I think this would be the best way to go."

"Why didn't you tell me about this option first and save all the time?" Sybil laughed.

"Presentation is everything…being in the business of beauty, you should know that."

"Indeed…continue."

"You can flip your own property. I know you say money is no issue, but why pay $100,000 for a house when you can get it for $50,000."

"Now you have my attention."

"Through my company, I can find you a foreclosed home in your preferred area of the city and remodel it to your liking. Instead of selling the property, you refinance out of the hard money loan into a traditional mortgage and keep it. You now have an investment property that can be

sold at market price if and
whenever you want to sell it."

Kevin continued to run
down the details of the flip option.
As he explained everything in
layman's terms, he noticed how
Sybil hung on his every word. It
seemed as his display of real estate
knowledge was turning her on.

"You've purchased a
property for $20,000 and put
$15,000 in it for the remodel. You
refinance $35,000 into a fixed rate
30 year mortgage and you have a
mortgage of about $120. On top of
that you have a property with a
market value a little over $100,000
depending on the area that you can
sell at that price. Now you have a
place you can stay anytime you
come to Atlanta."

"And if I sell the property
at market price I stand to make...,"

"A cool $65,000 depending
on how long you keep it. That's a

low end figure just to show you how everything works."

Sybil sat in silence for a good five minutes with her mouth open and a shocked look on her face.

"I had the same look on my face the first time my mentor broke it down for me," Kevin laughed.

"That is unbelievable. I must say…you know your business."

"The same thing you're doing for Brittany, my mentor did for me. Looking at how focused she is now reminds me of me when I first started out. You have truly been a Godsend for her."

"I'm passionate about what I do and I see that same passion in her. I'm sure it was always there…just hidden."

"It was a struggle in the beginning, but I tried to do all I could to break her from that dancer's mentality and focus on her future."

"You've done an excellent job with her. Not many men would do for his woman what you've done for yours. I can see her having the same success I enjoy if she continues on the path that she's on."

"I hope so."

"Before I decide to go with option three, could I possibly see those executive properties?"

"I'll call my guy to see if they're occupied. If they're empty, I can set up a time for you and him to meet and he can show you the properties."

"Well," Sybil hesitated. "Would it possible for you to show me the properties or at least be there with me? I have a few trust issues when it comes to meeting men I don't know."

"I assure you, Lonnie is a stand up guy."

"I don't doubt that, but I would still be more comfortable with you there."

"Say no more. I'll work it out."

"That's great," Sybil reached into her purse and pulled out a business card. "Here's all my information. Whenever you get it worked out, call me and we can set something up. I'm staying at the Westin downtown."

"I'll give Lonnie a call later on this evening."

"That sound's great. I look forward to hearing from you." Kevin stood up and escorted Sybil to her car. She opened the door then paused. "Listen, I know Brittany is your girlfriend, but can we keep my business ventures between you and I?"

"If that's what you want, I don't have a problem with that."

152

"Thank you. I'll talk to you soon."

7
Into Temptation

Steam filled the bathroom and fogged the glass door and walls of the standalone shower in the Master bathroom. Streams of hot water flooded and bombarded Kevin's muscular body as he rinsed the soap away. The lyrics and melody of Jaheim's classic ballad, *Put that Woman First,* floated from the speakers embedded in the ceiling. Soon the shower ended. Kevin dried his body with a plush navy blue towel then wrapped it around his waist. Brittany was stretched out on the bed working, ticking away on her laptop when he entered the room.

"You had a missed call while you were in the shower."

"Who was it?"

"There was no name. It was a 310 area code."

"310?" Kevin paused for a moment trying to think of where the area code was from.

"I think that's LA. I'm not sure."

"Who do I know that could be out in LA?"

"Could be anybody knowing you," Brittany giggled. "You probably got hoes in different area codes."

"You have no idea," Kevin laughed as he pulled an undershirt and boxer briefs from the drawer. "I used to have'em all over the country. I never told you about all the butt naked midgets I used to get freaky with."

"You are so nasty," Brittany playfully threw a pillow and hit Kevin in the head.

As the two went back and forth, Brittany's phone rang. When

she picked it up, she noticed it was the same 310 number that called Kevin.

"Somebody is calling me from the same number that called you."

"Answer it."

"I don't know who this is. You answer it." Brittany handed Kevin the phone. He swiped to accept the call.

"Hello?"

"May I speak with Brittany?" A familiar voice requested.

"Yes...may I ask who's calling?"

"This is Sybil."

"Hey, Sybil. This is Kevin."

"I just tried to call you."

"I'm sorry I missed your call. I was in the shower."

"You and I need to talk business as soon as you get a chance. Things have been so crazy since the last time we spoke. I had an emergency and had to fly out here to LA."

Brittany sat with a confused look on her face as Sybil and Kevin talked.

"That's no problem at all. If you like, I can give you a call as soon as I get to the office. That way I'll have everything in front of me."

"That sounds great."

"Here's Brittany. I'll talk to you in about an hour."

Kevin handed the phone to Brittany then walked into one of his closets. By the time the conversation was over, Kevin was coming out of his closet with black slacks on buttoning a dark grey shirt. After he got his shirt buttoned he sat down in his chair to put on his socks and shoes.

"What did Sybil want?"

"She was calling to tell me that she was sorry that she left without telling me and that she would be back to Atlanta next week."

"Oh, okay."

"Can I ask you a question?"

"Why was Sybil calling me?"

"Uhhhh…yeah."

"I can't get into any details about it because she asked me not to, but she came by the office last week and she needs my help with something."

"Why does she need your help?"

"It involves real estate."

"Why am I just hearing about this?"

"Because she asked me not to speak about it."

"To me?"

"To anybody. I know she didn't want to talk about the

business end of it, but I thought she would have at least told you she came by the office."

"She never mentioned it."

"I'm sure she had a reason."

"Why didn't you tell me she stopped by your office?"

"She asked me not to say anything."

"Since when do we keep things from each other?"

"Sweetheart, this is business. Some clients ask for confidentiality for whatever reason. I have to abide by that." Kevin noticed that Brittany did not have a pleasant look on her face. "Does it bother you that Sybil and I are doing business together?"

"The business is not the problem. The problem is that she went to my man's office and didn't tell me about it. She tells me everything else."

"Baby…calm down. I'm sure she has her reasons or it probably just slipped her mind."

"You don't understand how these females are out here."

Kevin saw the wheels in Brittany's head turning and felt that he needed to suppress all ill thoughts before they got out of hand. He walked over to the bed and pulled Brittany to her knees to face him. She wouldn't look him in the eye, so he placed his forehead to her forehead.

"Brittany Pricilla Hunter…I work with women all of the time. I never get involved with women I am in business with. I promise you…this is strictly professional. You are the only woman in my life and I can't buy you nice things or take you nice places if I don't make money. You do want daddy to make money, don't you?"

"Yes," Brittany replied in a low voice as she continued to look down. Kevin gently placed his hand on both sides of her face and lifted her head.

Looking her in the eyes, "I love you. I'll never do anything to intentionally hurt you."

A huge smile spread across Brittany's face. This was the first time that Kevin told her that he loved her.

"Do you really love me?"

"More than you know. You're my breath of fresh air when this crazy life I live consumes me sometimes. Just knowing that you're in my life, calms me."

Tears began to stream down Brittany's face.

"I love you too, Kevin. I've never had a man care for me and support me the way you do. I don't know where I'd be without you."

Kevin wrapped his arms around Brittany and squeezed her tight.

"You good?"

"I am now."

"Okay. I have to get to the office and get things together before I call Sybil back. Would you like to meet for lunch today?"

"I would love to, but we have a crazy day at school today. I'm free for dinner tonight though."

"Where would you like to go?"

"We're just going to be regular people tonight. We're not getting dressed up and we're not going anywhere fancy."

"You name the place and we'll go there."

"I've been craving seafood. Let's go to Spondivot's."

"Spondivot's it is. I'll see you when you get home."

Kevin kissed Brittany on her forehead and left the bedroom. He grabbed the keys to the Mercedes and was out the door.

———————————

A week later, Sybil returned to Atlanta. On a Wednesday afternoon, she met Kevin at his office to go view the executive properties before making her final decision. She called from the car to let him know that she was less than a minute away. Kevin met her in the parking lot.

"Kevin!" She greeted as she stepped out of the back of a black Lincoln Continental. "It is wonderful to see you again."

"Likewise. I have the keys to both properties. If you're ready, we can go."

"We can go now."

Kevin opened the passenger door to his Mercedes and helped Sybil into the luxury SUV then entered on the driver's side.

"I wasn't thinking when I left the house this morning. I should have driven something lower to the ground."

"I don't mind one bit. Besides, who complains about climbing into a Mercedes?"

"The first place I'll show you is the condo then we'll stop by the townhouse on the way back."

"Whatever is most convenient for you. I have so much trouble navigating in this city. That's why I hire a car service when I come to town."

"Atlanta isn't as difficult to navigate as you think. It didn't take me long to learn the city once I moved here. You learn quickly when you have to locate properties all over the city."

"I bet you do."

"I take it by today's visit you're leaning more toward the executive properties."

"I'm still on the fence, but I'm actually leaning toward having my own property. I just wanted to take a look to make sure."

"What type of home do you have in Miami?"

"I own a three bedroom oceanfront. I can walk out of my back door and onto the beach. I love it."

"I've always wanted to have a summer home on the beach in Florida."

"Well…until you make that happen, you're always welcome at my place."

Sybil's comment caught him off guard. When he looked over at her, she was looking straight forward with a devilish grin on her face.

"I appreciate the offer."

"Brittany tells me that you have business associates and investors in Miami."

I gave her my last breath.

"That's true. I'm working on a commercial deal with an investment group down there."

"What kind of deal?"

"There are a couple of strip malls that recently went into foreclosure. When the economy declined, it forced quite a few of the businesses out. We've just secured the land around one to expand it so that we can bring in what is called an anchor store."

"What is that?"

"Have you ever gone to Walmart and there are other stores and businesses around it?"

"Yes."

"Walmart is considered the anchor store because of its recognition. That will be the store that initially brings the most traffic to the area, thus allowing smaller, less known business to thrive."

"Oh okay…I understand now. Where will they be located?"

"One is in the Coral Gables area near the University of Miami and the other is near Hialeah."

"I've heard of those areas, but I'm not familiar with them."

"We have one obtained already and are close to closing on the other. We're going to remodel and restructure and sell to the highest bidder once we have commitments from the anchor stores."

"Sounds very lucrative," Sybil lulled. "There's something about a self-made man. He's the sexiest of all men as far as I'm concerned."

They continued to talk as they cruised down I-20 headed into downtown. Kevin continued to notice the slight sexual innuendos and comments Sybil threw his way. He did his best to dismiss them.

They arrived and viewed
their first destination. That took
about an hour of their time. Once
they were finished there, they
moved on to their next destination.
They pulled into a gated
community of gorgeous, brick
townhomes. Once at the one they
would be walking through, they
went inside. Sybil stepped out of
her shoes as soon as they entered
the foyer area of the townhome.

"I don't usually do this,"
Sybil began as she slid her shoes
together with her foot. "I bought
these shoes a tad bit small, but they
were the last pair and I had to have
them."

"I've done that a time or
two myself."

"Then you understand."

"Absolutely. Make yourself
at home."

Sybil admired the décor
and the overall architecture of the
structure. She marveled at the

hardwood floors, the windows and the size. She gasped when they entered the Master suite.

"This is unbelievable. It doesn't look this big from the outside. This is almost as big as my Master bedroom."

"Really? It think it's kind of small. The bed is a bit large for this room. I would have gone with a Queen."

Sybil lifted herself onto the bed and stretched out in order to test the mattress. The softness of the mattress along with the feel of the bedding caused her to moan as she rolled around in it. As she moaned, Sybil began to caress her own body in a manner that looked very sexual. Kevin stood and watched her.

"This feels like heaven," she moaned. "You have got to feel this."

"I'll take your word for it."

She reached up and released her hair from the ponytail it was pulled into. The visual was crucial. There lay a sexy woman with hair all over the place and a gorgeous body that was screaming to be touched. Not to mention the countless sexual faces Sybil made as she made eye contact with Kevin.

Kevin was a faithful man but nonetheless, he was still a man. Sybil's actions were beginning to turn him on. He had to figure out a way to get her out of that bed. As hard as he tried to come up with something, he kept coming up empty. Then it hit him.

"I need to make a call. Excuse me."

Kevin hurried downstairs and into the kitchen. He searched the cabinets until he found a glass.

In less than a minute he gulped down two large glasses of cold water. He leaned against the refrigerator and took deep breaths. By this time, Sybil made her way downstairs. Her hair was still wild and all over her face from her precious actions. She had unbuttoned her top three buttons allowing a generous amount of her ample bosom to be exposed.

"Is everything okay?" Sybil asked as if she had not just mentally raped Kevin.

"I'm fine. I was just a little thirsty. That's all."

"I'm sorry if I got a little carried away. That bed just felt so wonderful. Had I been in here all alone I would have taken off all my clothes."

"I see where you started," Kevin pointed out the buttons on her blouse.

"Come on, Kevin," she giggled. You act like you've never seen breasts before."

"I have…just not those."

While grabbing another button, "Would you like to see them? They're very nice."

"I'll take your word for it." Kevin looked at his watch. "Is it 2:30 already? I have to get back to the office."

"We really lost track of time. I have to be at the salon in an hour. Could you drop me off there?"

"Sure...not a problem."

The car was full of awkward silence as they rode back to Sybil's salon. He turned on the radio to break it. Once they arrived, he got out and helped Sybil out of the vehicle.

"Thank you for taking time out of your day to show me the

properties. I'll call you with my decision in the morning."

"That sounds great. I'll be waiting for it."

"One last question, if I choose to do my own property, can it be done similar to the townhouse?"

"I can do it any way you want."

"I was hoping you'd say that."

Sybil gave Kevin an evil grin and disappeared through the doors of her salon. Kevin climbed into his car, took a deep breath then exhaled before he finally drove off. Since he was in Buckhead, he decided to pay Rich a visit. He had to talk to someone about what just happened.

Rich was sitting in his office eating a sandwich when Kevin walked in. Kevin greeted his friend with a fist bump and sat down.

"What's wrong?" Rich asked as he wiped his mouth with a napkin. "You look like you've just seen a ghost."

"I didn't mean to interrupt your lunch, but I had to talk to somebody."

"What's up?"

"You remember me telling you about Sybil?"

"Sybil? It's not ringing a bell."

"She's the woman that's been mentoring my girl."

"Are you talking about the one with all the salons?"

"Yes…that's her."

"What about her?"

"She came to me and asked me for some help concerning real estate. She's either going to rent a property from one of my investors or she's going to do her own flip."

"So what's the problem?"

"She's been throwing a heavy sexual vibe at me ever since we first sat down to talk business. I took her to see the two properties she might be renting and it got very uncomfortable, very fast."

"I need a little bit more to go on."

"When we got to the second place, that's when it really went down. I'm showing her around and she's checking everything out. We get to the bedroom and she loses her mind. She gets in the bed and starts rolling around and touching herself like she's inviting me to get in the bed with her."

"Was she naked?"

"No, but had I made a move she would have come out of her clothes very quickly."

"Are you going to tell your girl?"

"That's what I'm unsure of. She's done some amazing things

for Brittany and can help her out a lot in the future. I don't want this to cause a rift between them. When it comes to the business Brittany wants to open and run, Sybil is the best resource for her to have."

"Look at it like this, when she was a dancer, men came onto her every night. Did she tell you about that?"

"No, but I feel that this is somehow a little different."

"How is it different? Whether a man comes on to her in the club or in the streets, it's her job to handle the situation and stay the course. If the situation rises and she's done all she can do and a guy won't leave her alone, that's where she brings you in."

"What about damage control? Suppose I keep ignoring her advances and she gets angry and tells Brittany the story, but the other way around…like it was me coming on to her."

176

"Your girl should know you better than that. Since you've been together, have you given her any reason not to trust you?"

"Of course not."

"Then that's a bridge you cross if you ever have to cross it. You and I both know how these women are. There is always something about a man, attached or not, that's about his business and getting money. Women come on to me all the time when they find out that this is my business. Men like you and I are rare in this city. They don't make'em like us too often."

"I don't know, man. I've worked too long and too hard to get things where they are between me and Brittany to allow somebody to come in and ruin it just like that. Do you know how long it took me to change her mentality?"

"I've gone through the same thing with Melissa and I'm

still going through it. Some women are tougher nuts to crack. Melissa's a work in progress."

"It's just a scary situation when it's someone that's so close to your other half. It's something about that unspoken bond that women have with each other when it comes to men."

"Listen to me. Calm down. I know it's a crazy situation, but you're going to drive yourself crazy if you dwell on it. You're a good brother and I trust that you'll make the right decision."

"You know what? You're right. I don't know why I'm trippin'."

"You're trippin' because all of this time you've been with Brittany, no one has tempted you. It was only a matter of time before it happened. You just have to be like Ali…float like a butterfly, sting like a bee."

"You a fool for that one,"
Kevin laughed.

Kevin left Rich's shop
feeling better about the situation.
He believed that he was a strong
man and could handle the situation.
If push came to shove, he would
have to let Brittany know what
Sybil was up to.

8
Bait

Three days after the uncomfortable encounter betwixt Sybil and Kevin, they found themselves face to face in Kevin's office to discuss Sybil's future business venture. She sat across from Kevin wearing a red satin blouse that was once again unbuttoned at the top allowing her cleavage to be on full display. The black skirt she wore extended to about three inches above the knee and hugged all of her lower assets. The top of Kevin's desk was glass so he had a bird's eye view of her long toned legs when she crossed them.

"Have you made your decision?" Kevin asked as he

leaned back in his black leather desk chair.

"I wouldn't be here if I hadn't."

"What did you decide?"

"I like the townhouse, but the one thing that turns me away from it is availability. I need a place that is there for me whenever I need it. I need to be able to have clothes there so I don't have to pack clothes for extended periods of time."

"I take it we're going with the flip."

"Yes. I took into consideration what you said about the amount of the mortgage and figured that I blow that kind of money on meaningless things. Why not put it into something of value?"

"I feel that you've made an excellent choice, but we need to get some things clear before we move forward."

"Like?"

"I believe in professionalism at all times with every client that I do business with. Our last encounter gives me reservations about moving forward with this venture. There's nothing wrong with a little harmless flirting, but I feel that a line was crossed."

"I apologize if I made you feel uncomfortable in any way. I've always been a huge flirt, but sometimes I do get carried away."

"To be honest, the only reason I bring it up is because of our mutual relationship with Brittany. She really looks up to you and is doing everything you tell her she should do in order to be successful. I don't want anything to jeopardize that. She has a bright future."

"I totally agree with you. Since we're being so honest, I have to clarify why I acted the way that

I did. You know that the business world has always been a male dominated field. When I first started out, the men that I needed anything from as far as getting my business off the ground, only saw me as a pretty face. I tried to keep it professional as long as I could, but I wasn't getting anywhere. When I changed the game and began to show a little interest in them and started doing a little flirting, doors where flying open faster than I could walk through them. When you have a dream, sometimes you're willing to do any and everything you can to see that dream come true, even if it meant sacrificing a little dignity for the moment."

"I don't understand why you felt that you needed to do that with me. I'm sure Brittany told you that I'm a paper chaser and for me, business is business no matter who it's with."

"I got that from you. I'm so used to turning it on when it is time to do business with a man, it has become second nature. It didn't help the situation with you being an attractive brother with his life together. Honestly, I envy Britany because she has a man like you and has the sense to hold onto him."

"I appreciate the compliment and I'm sorry that you've had to go through everything that you have to get to your current success. I know how some men can be especially when it comes to doing business with women."

"Can we just put that past incident behind us and move forward?"

"Indeed we can. I'm looking forward to it."

"Thank you for being so understanding. I promise that I'll behave."

"Now that we've gotten that out of the way, where in the city would you like me to locate a property for you?"

"Before I answer that, may I ask you a question?"

"Sure."

"Had you been a single man the other day, would you have joined me in that bed?"

"I'm going to exercise my right to plead the fifth on that one," Kevin grinned.

"Point received. By the way, I don't mind you telling Brittany about this business venture. All I ask is that you not disclose my finances."

"I can do that. I'm glad you're okay with it now because she's been bugging the hell out of me about it since we first talked."

Kevin and Sybil moved on in their conversation about their business venture. He got all the vitals and particulars out of the way and then got the contract signed. It was a good day, but Kevin still felt that the road ahead was going to be long and winding.

9
Optical Illusion

Over the next month, Kevin went through a grueling process of helping Sybil select a property in her area. It was obvious that she didn't understand the process of what was going on because every property Kevin selected for her was no good. When he was running out of options he had to sit her down and go over the entire process with her again. Once this was done, she finally selected one.

When the money was in place, the property was purchased. As he did for all of his projects, he selected a project manager and sent him to get the rehab started. When Sybil found out that Kevin wasn't managing her project, she insisted that he do so or she was going to pull the deal. At first it didn't matter to Kevin because he wouldn't be the one stuck with an unlivable property. In the best interest of business, he decided to find a way to fit it into his already hectic schedule. Little did he know, it was going to be more of a headache than he anticipated.

Sybil was at the project site everyday asking the same questions repeatedly. It was as if Kevin had a second shadow. Everywhere he turned, she was right there. During this process, Sybil went back on her word about behaving. It was a nightmare for Kevin. She constantly leaned over his shoulder while he was looking at things, pressing her soft breast against him. The sexual innuendos crept back in the conversation. Every evening when he called it quits for the day, Sybil invited him to dinner or back to wherever she was staying.

Any other man would have said "fuck it" and gave Sybil the long dick she was desperately searching for. Kevin couldn't bring himself to do that to Brittany. The thing that kept him going was the fact that by the time the project was over, Brittany will have finished school. By that time she will have built up all the contacts that she needed so that Sybil wouldn't have to be such a vital part of her life.

Friday rolled around and the work week was over. Kevin pulled into his driveway and dragged himself into the house. Brittany was waiting on him. The aroma of Italian meat sauce floated through the air. Kevin kicked his shoes off at the door and walked into the kitchen.

"Hey," he greeted in a tired manner.

"It's my baby!" Brittany squealed as she hugged and kissed her man. She noticed how exhausted he looked. "You look tired. Are you okay?"

"This project with Sybil is wearing me out. I'm not used to project managing like I used to be."

Kevin took a seat on a bar stool beside the stove. Brittany reached into the refrigerator, pulled out Kevin's favorite beer and poured it into a frozen glass that she took from the freezer.

"Thank you."

"Why isn't Clark or Diego doing it?"

"Diego is on another project and when I tried to give it to Clark, Sybil insisted that I do it."

"Doesn't she know that you're the CEO? Bill Gates doesn't build his own computers."

"I know, baby. You know how people can be with their first investment. They're so scared that something is going to go wrong."

"What about the project in Miami? Aren't you supposed to go next week?"

"Yes and I will be there. Clark is just going to have to fill in for me while I'm gone. The crazy thing is that I don't mind managing the project. The thing that bothers me is that Sybil is always there."

"Really?"

"She's annoying as hell."

"That explains why she's never available when I try to call her during the day and when I do get her, she says she has to call me back because all of the noise."

"To be honest, if it wasn't for you, I would have let her walk away from the deal when she threatened to pull out."

"Why did she threaten to pull out?"

"Because I told her that Clark was a capable project manager and that he could handle it. I didn't have to be there."

"Okay, but how did you stay in the deal because of me?"

"I didn't want to cause a rift between you two. You know how some women are. If something goes wrong between her and me, it would ultimately affect the two of you. I'm not saying that would have happened; I just didn't want to take that chance. You're so close to finishing school and she's a good resource for you to have moving forward with your business."

Brittany put the knife down that she was using to gut peppers and walked over to Kevin. She positioned herself between his legs and draped her arms around his neck.

"You are too good to me. I don't know many men that would sacrifice so much for me."

"I told you…when I'm with you, I'm with you. I only want what is best for you. If that means putting up with Sybil for a little while, then so be it."

Brittany smiled as she pressed her soft, full lips against Kevin's.

"Dinner is going to be about another hour and a half. Why don't you get out of these clothes, take a shower and I'll come in and give you a massage after I put the lasagna in the oven."

"That sounds like a plan. I'll be in the room when you're ready."

Kevin kissed Brittany on the forehead and headed to the Master bedroom. As Brittany continued to prepare dinner, the ding of a text message came through on Kevin's phone that was sitting on the counter. She tried to ignore it, but she couldn't. On Kevin's phone, the message appeared on the home screen. The text was from Sybil. It read: *I've really been enjoying our time together.*

A hundred thoughts raced through her mind as she read the text. Brittany began to wonder if Kevin had been lying to her about Sybil. She also pondered the fact of Sybil being in her face on a daily basis knowing that she was coming on to her man. Brittany didn't want to jump to any conclusions. She laid the phone back on the counter and continued to cook.

Because of all of the lies she has been told by men and all the cheating she has endured, she couldn't help but wonder what was going on. Kevin had been the ideal man for her, to this point. He couldn't possibly be hiding something. Could he?

———————————

The next week was not a good week for Brittany. The property that Sybil selected was in the same area as her school. On that Monday, she saw Sybil and Kevin ride by her school while she was sitting outside eating her lunch. She tried to call him, but he didn't answer. When she tried Sybil's phone, it went straight to voicemail. Knowing how hard it was for her to catch Kevin on the phone during the day, she dismissed.

Two days later, Brittany walked into her favorite deli around the corner from her school. Kevin and Sybil were sitting in there having lunch together. It looked like they were laughing and having a good time. She backed out unnoticed by either of the two. She called Kevin as she walked back to her school. He picked up.

"Hey babe," Kevin greeted while he was still laughing.

"How are you?" She asked surprised that he answered the phone.

"I'm sitting here with Sybil having lunch. What are you up to?"

"I'm on my lunch break, too. I'm trying to figure out what I want to eat."

"We're right around the corner from you at the deli you're always telling me about. Why don't you come and have lunch with us."

"I'm not that hungry. I think I'll just grab a bag of chips or something and read my book for the rest of my lunch break."

"Are you sure?"

"Yeah…I'm sure."

"I can bring you something by the school in case you get hungry later."

"I'll be okay. I just called to say hello. I'll see you at home."

"Okay, baby. I'll see you then."

"I love you."

"I love you, too."

A look of confusion fell on Brittany's face. How could anything be going on between Sybil and Kevin if he answered the phone, told her exactly where she knew he was and invited her to lunch? Those aren't the things that a man that's cheating does. Either he was telling the truth or he was putting on one hellavah front. Sybil knows about Brittany and Kevin. Some side chicks don't care. Brittany felt that if Kevin was keeping something from her, it had to be because she didn't tell him

what was going on the time she
started dancing again.

Brittany's mind was
playing so many tricks on her. It
seemed like everywhere she
looked, she thought she saw Kevin
and Sybil. She didn't want to
confront him, but she felt that she
needed to know what was going
on. The crazy thing about it was
that she didn't know if she would
believe him if he was telling the
truth.

The mind is a dangerous
thing. Prior to Sybil entering her
life, not once did she ever think
that Kevin was being unfaithful to
her. Now that she was doing
business with him, things seemed
to be different. When Kevin would
come home they laughed, talked,
played games, wrestled and other
fun things. Lately, those things
haven't happened between them.
He was always tired and often
cranky. When Brittany asked him

about it, Sybil was always the answer yet he takes her to lunch and it looks like they are having the time of their lives.

Unknowingly, Brittany's mentality was changing. The wheels of her mind turned like the gears inside a watch. Instead of confronting the situation and talking to Kevin about it, she decided to take a different approach to the situation.

Saturday night unfolded and the Atlanta night life was in high gear. Brittany and Kevin had plans to go out, but she broke them saying that some of her friends from school were going out for one of her classmate's birthday. Kevin didn't mind. He felt that he could find something to do on a Saturday night. He called Rich, but he didn't answer. Kevin decided to spend a relaxing evening at home.

I gave her my last breath.

Over in Buckhead, Rich sat with a couple of guys from his shop, drinking and laughing. He stopped in mid-laugh when he saw a familiar face walk in dressed in a skin-tight, backless, black dress that barely covered her backside and matching Stilettos. It was Brittany along with three other scantily clad women. The foursome found a table by the bar. Rich repositioned himself so that she couldn't see him.

Because of his allegiance to Kevin, he kept his eyes on Brittany. For the first part of the night, everything was cool. He watched as men approached the table and talked to the women. Brittany was cordial, but she didn't show interest in anyone or allow any man to linger with her for too long. That changed after a few drinks.

Around midnight a guy walked in by himself. He was

dressed in baggy jeans and an Atlanta Falcons jersey with matching hat. Brittany scooted off of the bar stool and greeted him with a hug then introduced him to the other ladies in attendance. The guy pulled up a chair from a nearby table and joined the ladies. Although there were three other women at the table, his focus was on Brittany.

Before jumping to any conclusions or making a scene, Rich sat back and observed. He noticed how she talked to him as if he were more than just a friend. She laughed at everything he said and constantly touched his arm and leg. Knowing that she was Kevin's girl began to anger Rich. She was not carrying herself or conducting herself in a way that says anything but single.

Thirty minutes later, Brittany and the unknown male left the bar together. Rich excused himself from his friends to follow them, but by the time he got outside, they had vanished into the crowd. Rich pulled out his phone to call Kevin, but it was dead. After everything Kevin has done for Brittany, Rich couldn't believe his eyes.

Since Brittany and Kevin started dating, Sunday was the day the couple always set aside for each other. With the perils and chaos of Kevin's work week and Brittany's focus on school, they always looked forward to their special day.

Brittany spent most of her nights at Kevin's. She slept in her own bed prior to going out with her girlfriends. That Sunday morning, Kevin went for his morning run then returned home to see when Brittany would be making her way to his place. Knowing that she went out, Kevin decided to wait until after noon to give her a call. His first attempt went straight to voicemail. He figured that she was still asleep.

After some light cleaning and straightening up his closets, Kevin gave Brittany another call. That call went directly to voicemail also. As he sat on his bed wondering why Brittany was not answering her phone, his doorbell rang. When he got to the door, it was Rich.

"To what do I owe this surprise visit?" Kevin asked as he greeted his friend. He noticed that Rich was not smiling. "What's wrong?"

"We need to talk. Is Brittany here?"

"It's just me. Come on in."

Kevin led Rich to his den and sat down on the sofa.

"I don't know how to tell you this, Kev."

"Tell me what?"

"I was in Buckhead last night and I saw Brittany."

"Yeah…she was out with her girls from school. She said something about celebrating somebody's birthday."

Rich paced back and forth in the den. He was trying to get the words together to tell Kevin what he saw the night before.

"I'm going to just come out and say it."

"Say what?"

"Brittany left the bar with another guy last night."

Rich's words hit Kevin like a shot of straight liquor. A look of confusion fell on his face. Kevin sat in silence for a good five minutes.

"Tell me the whole story."

Rich proceeded to tell Kevin how everything went down that he saw. He didn't leave out anything. Rich was thorough from the outfit she wore to the time that she left the bar.

"By the time I followed them outside, they were already out of sight. I'm not trying to be petty or start any confusion. I just thought you should know. I know you would do the same for me."

"Without question…"

Before Kevin could go any further, He heard the front door open and the beep of his alarm system. In a matter of minutes, Brittany entered the room.

"Hey baby," she hailed as she hugged Kevin from behind. "Hey Rich…how's Melissa?"

"She's doing well. I'll tell her you asked about her."

"I'm sorry I'm late. I left my phone in Stacy's car. I had to go by and get it. If you two will excuse me, I have to go and put my phone on the charger."

Brittany left the room.

I gave her my last breath.

"I guess that's my cue," Rich began as he reached out to shake Kevin's hand. "I'm sure you and your girl need to have a conversation."

"I appreciate you looking out."

"You're like my brother. That's what I'm supposed to do."

Rich let himself out as Kevin walked into the bedroom where Brittany was. She was propped up against the headboard looking through her phone.

"Who did you leave Shade with last night?"

"Excuse me?"

"You heard me. Who did you leave Shade with last night. What's his name?"

"Is that why Rich was here?"

"Answer the question, Brittany."

"Okay," Brittany took a deep breath then exhaled. "His

206

name is Shawn. We went to Clemson together. I hadn't seen him in a few years. He was in town and he asked if he could see me. I didn't know how you would react if I told you, so I asked him to meet me and the girls at Shade last night."

"Where did you go after you left Shade?"

"We went to this karaoke bar down the block."

"After everything we've been through," Kevin began with extreme volume in his voice. "Wait…I'm sorry. I'm not going to yell. We're grown."

"Baby, I'm sorry."

"That's the same thing you said to me after I found out you went back to dancing. Then you said it wouldn't happen again. Then you said you'd be open and honest with me. Where does this shit stop, Brittany?"

Tears began to roll down Brittany's face.

"You have to believe me. I didn't mean to keep that from you. It's just that…"

Brittany paused.

"It's just that what?"

"My mind has been buggin' these past couple of weeks. Ever since you started doing business with Sybil, my mind has been playing tricks on me."

"What are you talking about? What does Sybil have to do with this?"

"I've been feeling like there's something going on between you and Sybil?"

"Are you serious? Sybil is a client."

"I know, but she's always there. I see the two of you riding together. Remember the day I called you and you were at the deli with her? I know you were there with her. I walked in and saw you, but I turned around and walked back out. She's consumed all of your time. We don't talk like we used to. We don't do the fun stuff we used to do like play around and wrestle. Every night you come home, you're tired and cranky."

Kevin walked over to the bed and sat down beside Brittany.

"Why didn't you just talk to me?"

"Because my mind was so messed up, if you denied it, I probably wouldn't have believed you. You just don't understand what I've been through with men. You're the best thing that has happened to me in a long time, but all the lies and hurt aren't going to go away overnight. Things were good, but then I started to see the same pattern starting to happen again. You were distant, things were changing and I was feeling neglected."

"You know I'm not those other guys. Everything I do for you is because I love you. You are my world. I'm sorry if things haven't been the same since this whole Sybil deal has started. The same way you say that I don't understand the things that you've been through with men, is the same way you don't understand how draining it is for me to work with Sybil. I didn't want to tell you the things that have been going for fear that you'll lose out on a good business contact and resource."

"What's been going on?"

"Sybil tries me every chance she gets. She's been trying to wear me down, but I love you too much to fall for it. I have to grin and bear it because of the things she's doing for you. To be honest, I really think that's why she comes on so strong. She knows that I will just take it and not say anything."

Brittany's entire demeanor changed.

"Are you serious? You mean to tell me that this bitch is all up in my face smiling like nothing is going on and the whole time she's trying to get my man?"

"That's why I am the way I am when I come home. I'm mentally drained by the time I get here."

"This shit is going to stop. I almost ruined my relationship because of her. That's probably what she wanted the whole time."

"Are you going to say something to her?"

"The same sacrifices you've been making for me, I'm going to make them for you. I'm not going to say a word until this deal is done and you get your money. Until then, I'm going to drain her for everything I can get…business contacts, furniture and equipment wholesalers…the works."

"It feels so good to finally get that off of my chest. It was killing me."

"You just continue to do your thing and keep being the good man to me that you are. We'll get through this."

"I know this is all a misunderstanding, but there's still the matter of you not telling me about the dude from last night."

"Then we're even because you didn't tell me about what was going on with Sybil."

"I guess we are even."

10
Moonwalk

Every relationship has its ups and downs. Kevin and Brittany sure had theirs. As soon as Sybil fell out of the picture, things seemed to get better for them. Brittany was able to focus on school and finish. Kevin successfully added commercial real estate to his list of accomplishments. The deal he had in place in Miami netted him around $400,000. As promised, Kevin helped Brittany find her building and got her the necessary funding to get it renovated.

The Sanctuary opened in Buckhead that Spring of 2016. Armed with a crew of classmates and other industry professionals, Brittany was on her way to becoming a success in her own right. Through promotions, heavy marketing and connections, The Sanctuary was an instant success.

On a warm, May evening Brittany and Kevin were relaxing outside by the pool sipping wine and having conversation.

"Has it set in?" Kevin asked.

"Has what set in?"

"The fact that a few months ago you were just finishing school and now you are the owner of a successful spa."

"It's starting to. It just seems surreal to me. I never thought that this soon after school I'd be in this position. I always thought that I would have to work for someone else and save forever before I could open my own place."

"You really worked hard. This time last year you were you were a totally different person."

"I owe it all to you. Had you not come into my life, I'd probably still be at the club trying to figure out my next move."

"It's hard to step out of the box sometimes, even when you have a dream or idea you want to pursue. It's rough when you create a life for yourself and you still have to maintain that life."

"How do you mean?"

"Bills have to get paid. Rent has to be paid. It's hard to step out because you get comfortable. You know that chasing a dream isn't always lucrative in the beginning. Sometimes it takes someone to help you out and have your back when times get rough."

"I made a lot of money as a dancer, but I wasn't smart enough to put some of that away. I made sure my bills were paid and the rest was blown on clothes, trips and other things that I didn't need. I should have been in this position a long time ago."

"My father always told me that we live and we learn."

"That is so true. Mine used to say that life was the best teacher you'll ever have."

"Now that you're on your way, what's your next move?"

"For the business or for me?"

"For you."

"The first thing I'm going to do is get rid of that beat up Honda."

"I've been trying to buy you a car for the longest."

"I know, but some things I feel I need to do on my own."

"What's the use of me being successful if I can't share it with the woman I love?"

"You've done so much for me. It's time for me to start doing some things for you."

"That's not necessary. You continue to focus on the things that you want for you and the business. I'm okay."

"I have had my eye on this SLK250."

"Don't you think that's a bit much right now?"

"Says the man with a Maserati, a Benz and a Camaro."

"Those things didn't come to me in the first few months I was on my own. I drove a '95 Ford Explorer for the first two years I was in business. I could have bought a brand new car after my first couple of deals, but being in business for yourself can be risky. Just because it's good today, doesn't mean it'll be good tomorrow."

"So I'm just supposed to sit on my money?"

I gave her my last breath.

"I'm not saying that. You are the sole proprietor of The Sanctuary. That means you and you alone are responsible for everything. What if something happens to equipment? What if pipes burst? These are hypothetical situations, but they are things that can really happen. I'm just suggesting that you be smart with your money."

"I hear you."

Brittany's attitude changed. Everything that Kevin was telling her was true and for her benefit, but she was not trying to hear it. In her mind, she began to think that because Kevin had helped so much in the process of getting established, he thought that he could tell her what to do. That wasn't the case. Kevin was merely trying to help her make good business decisions.

The next day, Kevin arrived at Rich's shop for his weekly detailing. Rich was in his office when he got there.

"I'm glad you're here," Rich began as Kevin walked through the door. "Sit down. I want to show you something."

Rich reached into the top drawer of his desk and pulled out a small, Tiffany blue, velvet box.

"Is that what I think it is?"

Rich opened the box to reveal a huge diamond engagement ring.

"Three carat, princess cut solitaire with the two one carat diamonds on each side all set in platinum. What do you think?"

"The ring is hot, but are you sure?"

"I know Melissa and I have had our differences in the past, but we're good together. I'm ready. I'm going to ask her to marry me this weekend."

"If you're ready then I'm happy for you, man."

Rich noticed that the look on Kevin's face wasn't one of genuine happiness.

"What's the look for?"

"What look?"

"The look you have on your face right now."

"I just want you to be sure. Marriage is a huge step."

"But?"

"I'm just an outsider looking in so I don't know the full extent of the relationship between you and Melissa. I just don't think she's in the same place as you. I could be wrong. For your sake, I pray that I'm wrong."

"I know that we've had our problems in the past, but we're in a good place now. Can you just be happy for your boy?"

"You know what? I'm sorry. I'm truly happy for you."

"Thank you."

———————————

Later on that night, Kevin returned home. When he walked into his closet to take off his work clothes, he noticed that Brittany's closet was wide open…and empty. He walked into the bathroom. All of her belongings were gone. Confusion struck Kevin. He reached in his pants pocket and pulled out his phone to call Brittany.

"Hello?" Brittany answered.

"Is there something I should know?"

"Baby, before you get upset let me explain."

"I'm waiting."

"I just feel that I need to be on my own. I spend so much time at your place."

"I can understand that, but why not talk to me about it first?

Contrary to popular belief I am an understanding guy."

"I know. I just didn't want you to try to talk me out of it."

"Where is all of this coming from?"

"I've been feeling like this for a while. I just didn't know how or when to bring it up."

"Does this mean it's over for us?"

"It doesn't mean that at all. My feelings for you haven't changed. I just think that it would be better if I lived in my own space."

"Can I ask you a question?"

"Yes."

"Does this have anything to do with me telling you that I didn't think it is a good idea for you to buy a Mercedes right now?"

There was a long pause.

"I would be lying if I said that wasn't part of it. I just feel that as long as I'm there, you think you control me."

"Control you? Me controlling you would have been me telling you not to buy the Benz. I was merely giving you my professional opinion during a conversation we were having. You can do whatever you want. I was just trying to be helpful."

"You know what? You're right. Maybe it's just me. I've been so dependent on you since I left the club. Now that I'm in the positon I'm in, I just want to see if I can stand on my own two feet. Please tell me you understand that."

"Why not say that? All I've been is good to you since day one and you still don't feel you can sit down and talk to me when you have an issue…especially one involving me."

"Listen, Kevin. I know that I'm not perfect and like I've told you before, some wounds take longer to heal than others. You're absolutely right. You've been better to me than any other guy I've ever dealt with. I just need time to be in my own space and my own world. Is that asking too much?"

"You know what? That's fine. By all means, do your thing."

"Kevin don't be like that."

"Like what?"

"You're being very condescending right now. Nothing else is changing. I love you and I want us to be together. All I ask is that you support me in this decision like you've supported me in everything else."

"Okay….okay. If you feel this is something you need to do for you then so be it."

"This is not a permanent move, I promise. When things are where I need them to be in my life, we can get things back to where they were."

They finished the conversation. Kevin walked downstairs to his man cave and tried to escape from that moment. A barrage of assorted 90's R&B floated through the speakers as he lay on his couch, clutching a pillow and staring at the ceiling.

Kevin tried to replay his entire relationship with Brittany in order to find out where things went wrong. Even though she said that nothing had changed, he believed that when you take steps backwards, the demise in the relationship isn't far behind. While searching for answers, the only issue he found was the situation with Sybil but after that, things went back to normal.

11
The Beast…Unleashed

Time moved forward. Brittany and Kevin's relationship did not. Kevin understood the time consumption of getting a business off of the ground and running it successfully. When Brittany entered Kevin's life, it was still chaotic but he made time for her because he cared that much about her. Things changed drastically for the couple.

In the midst of the madness, Brittany regressed back to her old ways. Every Friday and Saturday night was spent out on the town with everyone that wasn't named Kevin. Sundays, the one day that they always set aside for each other, were being blown off. On several occasions, people that knew of Kevin and Brittany's relationship would tell him that they saw her with other guys.

Trying not to be the man that jumped to conclusions, he gave her every benefit of the doubt that he could. Kevin became that man that was oblivious to what was going on in his relationship…if that's still what you wanted to call it.

Phone calls began to go unanswered. The time between text replies were lengthening. The amount of words in the text messages were diminishing. Everything that Kevin had done for Brittany no longer had weight in the relationship. As each day passed, he felt more and more used. There was nothing anyone could do to help him out of his funk. The only one that could was nowhere to be found.

This is what happens when a man takes a chance and steps out of his comfort zone. Kevin knew that Brittany wasn't the type of woman he normally dealt with, but because his attraction was so strong for her, he took a chance. The way Brittany portrayed herself as *not being the average stripper* didn't help on the matter.

As the bond that held Kevin and Brittany together stretched to the breaking point, he felt that no one could understand his situation. He kept it to himself.

———————————

The sleek frame of Kevin's blue Maserati pulled into the parking lot of Rich's detail shop. He was hailed by everyone. On this day, Kevin wasn't his normal self. He spoke and was cordial but none of the usual banter and joking occurred. Kevin walked into

Rich's office and slumped in a chair.

"What troubles you, my brother?" Rich asked with deep concern for his comrade.

"I think I've lost her," Kevin replied while looking down at the floor.

"Who? Brittany?"

"Yes. The crazy thing is I don't know how and why."

"Have you talked to her?"

"I've called her, texted her, and left voicemails. I get no response."

"What happened?"

"I honestly couldn't tell you. One minute things are fine, the next thing I know, she moves out behind my back. She says that she needs some time to be on her own."

"Give her time. As good as you've been to her, she has to come around."

"I don't mind giving her space, but the last thing she said to me was that nothing has changed. A month has passed and everything has changed."

"I've been where you are right now. You have to believe me when I tell you that everything will work itself out in due time."

"What am I supposed to do in the mean time? Do I act like the last year and a half with this woman never happened?"

"I'm not saying that. All I'm trying to say is that you can't allow yourself to fall into a holding pattern while you wait on her. Life is too short. You have to live."

"I was living. I was living with Brittany in my life. I knew I shouldn't have taken the chance on her. I should've stayed in my comfort zone."

"Comfort zones are good sometimes, but often times you have to shake things up. You've

230

done that with business and again with Brittany. Nothing in life is guaranteed. We both know that. If she doesn't have the sense to realize what she has then it's not on you. You've done all you can do."

"That's just the thing. I did everything for her. I took her out of the strip club. I helped her get her life on track. I helped her get a job so she could support herself while she finished school. I even helped her get her business off of the ground. After all of that, what do I have to show for it besides a broken heart?"

"You say that like you've already given up and accepted defeat. If you feel that strongly about her, then it's time for you to lay all of your cards on the table with her."

"And do what? Propose?"

"I'm not saying that. You need to sit her down and have a

face to face conversation.
Everything you want to say to her,
say it. Don't hold anything back.
Let her know how you feel. Then
you let her know that the ball is in
her court. She's either going to
play ball or pass."

"That sounds a little risky."

"She either wants to be
with you or she doesn't. You can't
allow her to make you put your life
on hold while you wait on her.
That's not fair to you."

Kevin stood up and took a
deep breath. He thanked his friend
for the advice. They continued to
talk while his car was being
finished. Once it was complete, he
left the shop.

It was around two o'clock
in the afternoon when Kevin
arrived at The Sanctuary. When he
entered, he began to see the looks
on the faces of some of the women
that worked there. It was the look

of someone that has just seen a ghost. The receptionist was new. She had no idea who Kevin was.

Kevin inquired about Brittany's whereabouts. Without knowing, the young lady informed him that Brittany had already left for the day because she was feeling ill. He thanked her and left. Kevin got back into his car and headed to her apartment in Cobb County to make sure that Brittany was okay.

Traffic was starting to get thick just as he neared Brittany's place. Kevin pulled up just in time to see an unfamiliar male exiting her apartment. He sat in his car until the stranger got into his car and drove off. Needless to say, Kevin was heated.

Kevin slammed the car door when he got out and walked with extreme swiftness up to Brittany's door and knocked. Brittany must have thought it was the other guy returning.

"Did you forget…?" All of the color left her face when she saw that it was Kevin standing on the other side of the door. "Kevin…what are you doing here?"

Kevin walked past Brittany and into her living room.

"You know," Kevin began as he laughed, "life is a funny thing. I haven't talked to my girl in almost a month so I decide to drop by her place of business because I was in the neighborhood. When I get there, you're not there. I was told that you went home early because you were sick."

"I was…"

"Please don't interrupt me right now. That's rude. Thank you."

Kevin's calm demeanor and tone of voice began to scare Brittany. She tried to grab her cell phone off of the coffee table, but Kevin grabbed it before she could.

234

"Kevin you're scaring me."

"I was told that you went home early because you were sick. Being the loving and caring boyfriend that I am and have always been, I travel across the city of Atlanta to come here and make sure you're alright. Normally, I would have called to check on you, but since you haven't picked up the phone nor returned any of my calls or texts, I decided to just come on over."

"Kevin, let me explain."

"I asked you not to interrupt me. I have something I need to say to you and DAMN IT-- YOU'RE GOING TO LISTEN!"

Kevin threw Brittany's cell phone into the wall and watched it shatter into pieces. Brittany backed up and cowered on the couch. She had never seen Kevin this angry before. She didn't know what he would do so she sat quietly and listened.

"I pull up just in time to see some strange man coming out of my girlfriend's apartment. Being that I have not seen nor heard from you in a month, that is leading me to believe that some really foul shit is going on. I'm going to ask you one time and you better not lie to me. Who is he?"

Brittany sat in silence.

"ANSWER ME!" Kevin barked causing Brittany to flinch.

"He's the guy I've been seeing," Brittany replied as tears began to stream down her face.

"Just cut it out. It's not going to work this time. The last time I caught you in some shit, you turned on the water works and I caved. It's not happening this time. How long have you been seeing him?"

"Four months," Brittany mumbled.

"Speak up. I can't hear you.

"Four months."

236

"Four months….Wow. So you've been playing me all of this time. All of this time, I thought I was in the perfect relationship with a woman that I love. Did you know that since we first got together, every morning when I woke up, I thanked God for sending you to me?"

"I never meant to hurt you. After that whole mess with Sybil…"

"That's what this is all about? Sybil? I told you how I fought off her advances because of you. How I could have screwed her brains out every day during her project, but I didn't because of you. I put up with her because I didn't want you to lose out on an excellent business resource and contact. I'm punished for a crime I didn't commit?"

"You never slept with Sybil?"

"No! Why would I sleep with Sybil? You were the woman in my life."

"She told me the two of you were together on a few occasions. I didn't want to believe it, but the way things were looking I couldn't help but believe it. That's why I moved out."

"And you believed this bitch over your own man? After everything I've done for you?"

"I can't believe she ruined my relationship."

"She didn't ruin your relationship. You ruined your relationship. You want to know how and why? Because whenever something came up you acted like you couldn't talk to me about it. First the debt owed to J-Rock and then Sybil. You can't put any of this on anybody but yourself."

"But you were trying to control me."

"How was I trying to control you? Because I said it wasn't a wise decision to buy a Mercedes right now? Grow the fuck up. You're a grown ass woman. You could've done whatever you wanted to do. I was just trying to give you helpful advice from one business person to another."

"What about all of the expensive things you bought for me?"

"I bought things for you from my heart and never once asked or expected anything in return. Most guys wouldn't buy you Dolce, Vera Wang, Prada, or Chanel because they don't have it like that. Newsflash: I have it like that! What do I look like stepping out in Alexander McQueen and the lady on my arm has on some bullshit from the Express? I did those things because I cared for you just that much. I didn't have to, but I did."

Brittany stood up and walked over to Kevin and tried to put her arms around his neck. Kevin grabbed her arms and removed them. Brittany kept trying to hug Kevin as she sobbed uncontrollably. He finally grabbed her firmly by her arms but not too firm as to hurt her and shook her once."

"Stop it!" He let her go. Brittany flopped back down onto the couch. "I gave you everything. I helped you get out of the strip club. I helped you bet back on track so you could fulfill your dream. I paid debts for you. I stood beside you. I was understanding as you transitioned. I watched you walk across that stage and I was there when you cut the ribbon at your grand opening. Watched you grow as a woman. I did all of that and the only thing I ever wanted in return was for you to be honest with me and love me like you said you did, but you couldn't even do that."

"Baby, I'm so sorry. You have to believe me."

"I believe you. You know what else I believe?" Brittany looked up at Kevin. Her face was flushed and soaked with tears. "I believe that never again will I allow myself to be played the way you played me. Now I'm starting to believe that I was the golden goose. You saw me that night and saw sucker written all over my face. Like a dumbass, I fell for it. Never again."

Kevin turned is back on Brittany and walked out of the apartment. She rushed to the door calling for him and begging for him to come back. Unlike Lot from the Bible, Kevin didn't look back.

He hopped in his car and sped away.

Once Kevin merged onto I-285, he reached into his console and pulled out his phone. After scrolling through the contacts, he found the number he was looking for. He tapped the green telephone icon to dial the number. A familiar voice floated through the speakers of the car.

"Hello stranger," the voice answered.

"What's up, Sybil. How you been?"

"I've been well…missing you, of course."

"That's actually why I called."

"Really?"

"I'll be in Miami this weekend. I'd love to see you. We have some unfinished business that we need to attend to."

Thank you for reading the first installment of **Pulsations of A Heartbeat**: *I gave her my last breath*. I hope you enjoyed it and be sure to check out installment two, **Pulsations of A Heartbeat**: *Unholy Matrimony* by fellow Author, *Antwan 'Ant' Bank$*. Please don't hesitate to leave a review on my Amazon or Barnes & Noble comment forums. I would love to hear from you! If you want to contact me directly, you may do so via Printhousebooks.com

I gave her my last breath.

Other titles available from this Author:

Silhouettes of two lovers are cast upon the walls by the flickering light of the spiced apple scented candles. The ambiance is intensified by the soothing voice of your favorite songbird. Chocolate dipped strawberries and champagne on ice are the chosen consumptions for the occasion. As you pull away the bitten strawberry from the lips of your lover, you gaze into his eyes. A warm sensation fills your body because you now feel that you have found your soul mate. If you could look deeper into those eyes you love so much, you would not find the love you've been so desperately seeking. You would find a hidden agenda masked by what you thought was true love.

I gave her my last breath.

There once was a time where if you wanted to talk to someone, you picked up your landline and called them. If that person wasn't home, you had to wait until they were. In that same time, if you wanted to meet a man or a woman, you went out to a club or a bar. While at the bar, you would survey the room until you found someone that caught your eye. When that person was identified, the next step was to build up the courage to approach that person or wait for an opening. From that initial meeting came different outcomes: rejection or acceptance. If acceptance was the outcome, you exchanged numbers and the courtship began. The courtship included a series of phone conversations—some filled with plenty of awkward breathing. Also in the courtship there was a series of dates and meetings until the two people involved came to a mutual understanding that it was time to move to the next level…the relationship and all that follows.

I gave her my last breath.

PRINTHOUSE BOOKS.

Read it, Enjoy it, Tell a friend.

**VIP INK Publishing Group,
Incorporated.**

Atlanta, GA.

www.PrintHouseBooks.com

www.ingramcontent.com/pod-product-compliance
Lightning Source LLC
Chambersburg PA
CBHW072350020726
47506CB00004B/1082